All Roads

Holly Schindler

All Roads

Published by Holly Schindler, LLC

Copyright © 2017 by Holly Schindler

This is a work of fiction. Names, characters, places,
and incidents are either the product of the author's
imagination or are used fictitiously, and are not to be
construed as real. Any resemblance to actual persons,
living or dead, business establishments, events, or
locales is entirely coincidental.

Cover and interior design by Holly Schindler

Cover images by Jaromir Chalabala and agrofruti,
courtesy of Shutterstock

Marzipan font by ForgottenRiver, courtesy of Etsy
Luna font by ORCA Creative Store and Loveline
Brush Script font by Pink Coffie, both courtesy of
Creative Market

May the road you're
traveling
be the same
that
leads you home.

Jesse

The General jumped through the rolled-down window before Jesse could stop him. It all happened in a single fluid lurch, his body curving over the edge of the passenger door of their '97 Winnebago as beautifully as a horse clearing a hurdle. And then he was galloping across the street, zipping toward the fold of the horizon.

But why? The General had given no hint that he was currently unhappy with his situation. When they'd pulled into the gas station, he'd still been wearing that goofy ecstatic-to-be-with-you tongue-dan-

All Roads

gling grin. Jesse had learned dogs really did have fa-
cial expressions—though nothing could beat the one
he'd worn the day they'd met, The General fearlessly
trotting up to Jesse's side. Dirty enough to proclaim
he'd been a stray too long for his owners to still be
looking, The General had cocked his head, wiry hair
lifting from his neck to expose a cloth collar embroidered with his name. He'd raised his eyebrow at Jesse
as if to say, "Well? How about it? You need a traveling
companion, and I'm tired of bumping around out here
by myself."

A dark pit dug itself into Jesse's stomach as
he watched The General grow smaller. Strange—he
hadn't spent ten minutes of his twenty-four years feeling sentimental about anything. And yet, the idea of
losing The General completely in a little less than two
weeks sent pure panic through him, a vicious repeating
stab.

Why would he want to escape? Jesse'd opened
his house-on-wheels to him, fed him, bathed the gunk
off of him, allowed him to sleep beside him in bed.
Turned him from a stray into a wanted dog, a loved
dog. Why would he give that up? Trash the good thing
he had going—for what? To chase a squirrel? What

2

could have possibly snagged his attention?

Jesse raced in the same direction, blowing furiously on a dog whistle. His cheeks puffed and his face grew hot in desperation as he ran straight for a small-town square—gazebo, grass, gossip, and gambling every Bingo Tuesday at the Elks Lodge, in full view of City Hall. Even as he sped by, the quaint simplicity looked shamelessly fake to Jesse, like a play backdrop.

"Where have you been, you naughty thing!"

The voice was female, young, and coming from the sidewalk that stretched before a plate glass window branded, proudly, "Katy's Kitchen." And it was being directed right at The General.

Jesse heaved a relieved breath. He dropped the whistle into the pocket of his zippered sweatshirt, too relieved to question why the whistle hadn't worked for the first time in more than a week of regular use. He clapped his hands and shouted, "Come on, boy! Let's go!"

Ignoring Jesse—or maybe assuming he was calling out to someone else—the woman squatted and began to rub The General's long ears. With each tug, the dog's face shifted deeper into an expression of pure ecstasy. To pry him free now would take nothing short of a miracle. Or one of those fake-bacon dog treats he'd been gobbling up.

"Sorry," Jesse apologized, looping a finger under The General's new collar, the one he'd bought along with the dog whistle, made of nylon and guaranteed for durability. A sturdier, more suitable collar. No embroidered name this time. Somehow, in Jesse's mind, a dog's name was kind of like knowing the combination to a safe—proof of ownership.

"Sorry for what?" the woman asked. "You brought The General back."

Jesse recoiled. Was she a fortune teller? A psychic? No way could she have guessed such a strange name. "That's my dog," he insisted. And repeated himself when she didn't respond.

"He got away from me when I was making a delivery," she offered, paying far more attention to The General than to Jesse's declaration of ownership. "Where've you been, you crazy boy? Feels like decades since I saw you." She wrapped her arms around his neck in a hug. For emphasis, she added a few pitiful squeaks to illustrate the heartache she'd been feeling.

Jesse trembled. This couldn't be her dog. It just couldn't. He and The General had crossed paths close

4

by, but he hadn't seen a single "Lost Dog" poster hanging anywhere. And besides—*far too dirty for his owners to still be looking.* Jesse frowned at The General in an accusatory way, like somehow, the dog had purposefully deceived him. Sheesh. As dirty as The General'd been when they'd met, Jesse'd actually wondered if the poor guy hadn't been walking for a hundred-plus miles.

It might answer the question of why The General had leapt from the RV, though. He wasn't escaping Jesse so much as he was running home.

The entrance to Katy's Kitchen swung open and an older woman stepped outside, white chin-length hair flying about her face, white Styrofoam containers in her hand.

"Looky who decided to come home," the woman said. She glanced behind her shoulder, rapped her knuckles on the Katy's Kitchen plate glass window.

A middle-aged woman (graying blond hair, wrinkles like only the fair-skinned collected, deep enough to be visible from a distance) stopped clearing a nearby table long enough to look at the small crowd that had gathered on the sidewalk. She grinned, pointed at The General, and gave an enthusiastic thumbs-up. "Yay!" she cheered.

All Roads

Did everyone in town know this dog?

The older woman smiled at The General, then eyed Jesse. "That's my daughter, Katy," she explained, gesturing toward the woman behind the glass, who had returned to clearing tables. "Louisa's my granddaughter," she went on, nodding at the woman still squatting in front of The General. "And I'm Betsy. And for the life of me, I couldn't tell you which one of us is happier to have this guy back."

As though to make her case that she was hands down the most grateful, Louisa began to kiss The General's right ear, tiny little pecks repeating over and over, like she was determined to give him one kiss for each day they'd been apart.

"You've got this wrong," Jesse insisted.

Betsy cocked her head to the side. "I'm sorry. I thought, the way you were standing here talking to Louisa—I assumed—you're the one that found him and brought him back, right?"

Jesse shook his head violently. "No. I mean, he came with me, but I'm not going to...He's mine."

Louisa finally let go of The General and stood, propping her hands on the hips of her baggy jeans. She shook her head, ridding her eyes of the strands

6

that had slipped from her blond-streaked mess of a braid.

"You're the one that's got it all wrong," Louisa snapped. "I raised him from a pup. I *adopted* him. From the local vet who found him abandoned on his door-step. I took him in. Me."

She drew out that word—*adopted*—like it should have had some sort of special impact. Which seemed a bit ridiculous to Jesse. How else did a dog come into a person's life? *Rescue*, Jesse remembered—that was the other word that people liked to use for their animals. Especially those given-up-on dogs at animal shelters. *I rescued him*, those words pinned to their chests like Boy Scout badges or Medals of Honor.

Or did adoption mean something specific when it came to dogs? Did she have some sort of legal papers?

"What did you say your name was, son?" Betsy asked.

"Jesse," he croaked. "Smith."

Betsy's eyes bounced all over him—face, shoulders, hands. It seemed she stared for the longest time at his hands, that they were of the most interest to her. Why? Did she expect him to be holding something?

7

All Roads

Was she checking to see if he was armed? Or simply reading his body language? Did it mean something, the way he was standing? A man who didn't put his hands in his pockets. Couldn't she take that as some sort of sign that he had nothing to hide?

He tried to hold himself steady, but his nerves got the better of him, and his eyes began to flutter. It was an old tic that had followed him from childhood, that he'd never quite outgrown: a short period of rapid blinking, his eyelashes flapping like hummingbird wings.

He shook his head once and placed his fingers on both eyes, waiting for the twitch to calm down.

And steeled himself against what was sure to come—the sound of the women sending him away. Shooing him like the stray he'd obviously mistaken The General for.

"Well," Betsy finally said, her voice laced with a kind of old-fashioned twang, not quite Southern, and rarely heard outside of old Sunday afternoon classic Western movies. "You'd best hurry up."

"Hurry?" Jesse asked. Was she serious? "Where?"

"Home, of course."

Jesse swallowed both his shock and a laugh. His home—or the closest thing he'd ever had to one—was back at the gas station. *Foster kid*; did you ever outgrow it? He would surely never forget the last day in the system, standing in the yard of the double-wide trailer the county had chosen to be his home for his teenage years. The trailer had always smelled like newspapers to him, like something you only needed the very moment it arrived, and then you trashed it, because come on, it was never meant to be given a special permanent place. There'd been a slap on the back of the shoulder from his chronically disinterested foster father that last day, an *'atta boy*, though for what, Jesse hadn't known. He'd achieved nothing but his eighteenth birthday, hardly a feat of anything but breathing in and out every single day.

And money. There'd been money, too. Gathered up in his name at the fosters' church. "To give you a leg up," or so the card had said. Funny, he'd thought then, how some folks thought cash could solve so much—buy forgiveness, maybe, scrub away so many injuries or mistakes.

Still. Cash. It was an idea, anyway. Especially with that word *adopted* hanging in the air. Maybe they needed a formal exchange. "How much for me to keep him?" he asked.

"How much?" Louisa echoed, her tone saturated with disgust. "You don't just go buying somebody else's dog."

"Now, now," Betsy said, putting a hand on Louisa's shoulder.

Louisa flinched and attacked the purse she was wearing—one of those with a long strap that draped across her body at an angle. And began to dig at the contents furiously.

"Don't get in a huff," Betsy tried. "That man took good care of The General. Look at him. New collar, well fed. Had a bath or two, surely. And you and I know how much patience that took, since The General is a full-time, professional bath hater. Grew quite fond of him, judging by that look on his face."

Louisa tugged a leash, rubber-banded into a coil, from the depths of her enormous, floppy purse. Furiously, she snapped it to the collar Jesse had bought.

Betsy frowned. "We owe the man a slice of hospitality and a nice meal at the very least, don't you think? Got plenty home cookin' to go 'round." She lifted the Styrofoam containers higher into the air to

10

illustrate.

Louisa's shoulders collapsed, making her look like a little girl being scolded. And she nodded once, relenting to Betsy's suggestion.

"Well?" Betsy asked The General. "Who you ridin' with, boy?"

This was getting decidedly weird. And strangely hopeful. Maybe, Jesse thought, he could convince The General to ride with him to wherever the women wanted to take him. And then he could kind of fall behind, take a different turn, be off to another town.

He expected this thought to come as relief. Instead, he felt it again—the repeating stab, every bit as vicious as it had been before. The strange part was, it wasn't guilt that he was feeling. It was loss. Again. Even though, in the scenario he'd just imagined, Louisa would be the one on the losing end. He felt her own potential loss as though it were his own.

He tried to peel it away, whatever it was that he'd suddenly begun to feel for the girl. Sympathy? That didn't seem quite right. But he didn't have time, right then, to figure it out, either.

With his heart beating a relentless, earsplitting bass line and his hands trembling, Jesse patted

11

All Roads

his leg, whistled. He wished The General was not a nearly-hundred-pound, probably Labrador / Golden Retriever mix. Some sort of terrier—now, there'd be a breed he could tuck under his arm and carry back to the Winnebago. No convincing needed.

Frankly, Jesse wasn't sure he *could* convince The General. Where were the dog's loyalties? Who did he love more? What did he consider his true home? Could two measly weeks be enough for anyone—man or dog—to ever call a location by that name?

The General flashed a pleading look at Jesse before turning to follow Louisa as she made her way down the sidewalk.

"I need directions," Jesse blurted.

"No, you don't," Betsy called as she rushed to Louisa's side. "All roads lead there."

"To where?" Jesse pleaded.

"Home. I told you," Betsy said, flashing him an easy smile.

Louisa

"**P**retty disappointed in you," Betsy said, her words jiggling as the pickup bounced down the dirt path.

Louisa cringed; even now, a word of disapproval from her grandmother could make her feel eight years old again, sorry and ashamed of her own behavior. But instead of nodding an apology, as Betsy surely wanted her to do, Louisa only began to scratch The General behind his floppy blond ear.

When her fingers hit the stiff nylon of his new collar, Louisa squeezed the plastic clasp open, slipped it from his neck. What had happened to the nice, soft collar she'd made? The General started kissing her cheek as though to thank her—maybe for freeing him from the collar, maybe for the ear-rub—as she leaned forward to slam the stranger's purchase in the glove compartment.

"Why'd you have to go and invite him over?" Louisa grumbled, eyeing the RV in the rearview mirror.

"Why'd I—he took care of The General! Every single day he's been with that man, he was The General's family!"

Louisa clenched her jaw, grinding her teeth together to keep her protests from slipping out. She didn't like the way that Betsy seemed to so easily—even, at times, sloppily—throw that word around. *Family.* A hugger and a woman with a perpetual open-door policy, Betsy used the word to describe both Louisa and Louisa's boyfriend—even though there had not yet been talk of a ring. In another few days, when she made her yearly Thanksgiving toast, she would use that word to describe both Louisa's mother and her mother's best friend, the old college roommate who always brought her famous hot rolls. She used it to describe the Pendleton family that lived across the street, the

14

pharmacist who sold her diabetes test strips, and even the most loyal customers who frequented the shop she and Louisa ran together.

To Louisa, though, pinning that word on so many people cheapened it, watered it down. As far as Louisa was concerned, "family" was a heavy word; it was permanent and valuable. She used it rarely, believing it only applied to her mother, grandmother, and The General.

Well. The term actually applied to one other person, too. James. Her long-absent twin brother.

Louisa rubbed the purple birthmark on her wrist as she said, "You don't know anything about him. This Jesse guy. What kind of person is he? Does he really love The General? Or did he want him for protection out there? Why? What kind of stuff's he into if he needs protecting? Maybe he's not on the up-and-up. And here you are showing him where we live."

"Oh, *really*—" Betsy moaned, as if Louisa had just recited a regular conspiracy theory.

"What if he comes with a bunch of ulterior motives?" Louisa asked.

"Like what?"

"Like anything. Robbing us."

All Roads

"You and I already went to the bank to make our daily deposit. Right after we closed."

"He doesn't know that. Besides, once he knows where we live, he could come back at any time. Wait for us to go to sleep, then barge in, demanding money. What if, one night, while you and I are watching TV, he opens the gate to the backyard and calls The General back into that Winnebago of his?"

"Louisa!" Betsy shouted.

"We know nothing about him. Why's he drive that RV?"

"He was probably camping."

"We don't have an RV park in town. The General went missing two weeks ago. Has he been here that long? Two weeks he's been bouncing around without going home? Does he live in that RV? Why? Kind of unusual for a young guy like that, isn't it? Who does that? Someone who needs to hide?"

"I'm telling you, he's not a thief."

"How do you know?"

"I just—I know. I saw it in him."

Louisa shook her head.

"Not everyone is out to steal something. Not like—"

Like your father, Louisa knew Betsy wanted to finish. But she didn't. She left the sentence without an end—which was actually how Louisa usually thought of her father: unexplained, unknowable, incomplete.

"I hope you're right," Louisa said, "but I'm afraid."

"Best thing we could do for you, young lady, is come up with a few exercises in trust," Betsy observed, swerving into their usual spot.

The Winnebago pulled into the parking space beside them.

"I thought you said home. Isn't this—a shop?" Jesse asked, his face turned toward their yard sign: "A Stitch in Time."

"Home, studio, and shop—all of the above," Betsy proclaimed happily.

"Maybe it's not New York or L.A.," Louisa started, feeling a little defensive. "Maybe it seems a little strange for a mid-sized town in Missouri, but we're not the only ones. This entire neighborhood is the Blue River Creative District." *Much admired creative district*, she could have added, but it felt like horn-tooting. And besides, wouldn't that lead Jesse to think their stuff was incredibly valuable?

All Roads

She tried to offer a pleasant smile. She wanted to seem relaxed and calm about welcoming this Jesse person. Like it was no big deal. Sometimes, she knew, people lived up to your worst expectations—better not give Jesse any bad ideas.

Meanwhile, The General was galloping up toward the front door like a child who'd been on an extended summer vacation, anxious to crawl into his own bed and revisit the toys he'd left behind.

"Work, display, sell all in the same place," Betsy added. "Right within walking distance, we've got potters, photographers, painters…"

"And you guys—what exactly do you—" Jesse started, but the moment Betsy ushered them inside, it was obvious. A textile shop: yarns and fabrics galore. His words halted as he drank it all in. Their shop was awash in color; it pulsed with zigzag patterns and plaids and polka dots.

"We print fabric for designers—mostly interior decorators. I do some weaving. Louisa does a lot of spinning." Betsy pointed at the large wooden spinning wheel where Louisa sat for hours each day, turning raw wool into yarn.

"Somethin' almost magical about turning a single thread into a giant piece of fabric," Betsy went on. But it wasn't just about making something with visual appeal, either. Betsy often said she saw no purpose in making pretty things that had no function. And never did a customer admit that they had put some of Betsy's linens away "for good" without a friendly but pointed tongue lashing. Betsy didn't want her creations shunted to the guest closet forever. She wanted her rugs to get stomped on and her pillows to get stained. She wanted life smeared all over them—that was how she'd often phrased it.

Yes, life was messy. Love was messy. Family was messy, too.

Louisa flinched a bit when that thought found her. She didn't really like the word "family" popping into her head with a meddling stranger standing so close.

Louisa and Jesse followed Betsy as she hurried out of their shop and through their living area. The General bounded out through the back door that Betsy flicked open, galloping through seed-laden fall grass, surely heading straight for the small creek that bordered their property. One of his all-time favorite spots.

Jesse let out a little noise of—what was that? A

19

whimper? At any rate, he seemed to be asking how the women could let The General run off less than fifteen minutes after he'd finally come home.

"Don't worry," Betsy told Jesse. "He'll be back. Especially for dinner. Just got to patrol the premises first." She gestured in a way that insisted, in the meantime, they all enjoy this little slice of heaven: the well-manicured square of a back lawn that gave way to lush tree-lined fields, more than three acres.

This was maybe Louisa's favorite part of their workplace—and the area where she came to recharge. There was something about an uncultivated field that seemed healing to her, somehow. Good for the soul. Plus, she liked the unexpectedness and hidden-away-ness of it, a slice of the country mere feet from the strip of stores, business signs, white lines drawn into the street for customer parking.

"Wow," she thought she heard Jesse mutter.

She softened toward him a little then. Felt calm enough to take a big inhale.

"Hungry?" Betsy pointed Jesse toward a picnic table set up beneath a patch of burgundy-leaved dogwood trees and covered with a muslin cloth, the corners secured against the sweet autumn breeze with antiqued brass tacks. She flipped open her Styrofoam containers, exposing piles of fried chicken and biscuits. New potatoes and peas, and slices of a glistening peach lattice crust pie.

She dashed back inside to retrieve a pitcher of iced tea.

"Hard to believe we can still eat out here—have an actual picnic—so late in the year. Almost all the way to Thanks and giving," Betsy said, plopping the pitcher in the center of the table.

Louisa chuckled. That was the way Betsy always said it: *Thanks and giving.*

"The leaves are finally turning—which is nice—but you should see this place in the peak of wildflower season," Betsy went on.

Louisa was still smiling slightly as Jesse reached for his glass. But her smile broke into a grimace when Jesse brushed against her, sending a fresh lightning bolt of pain up her arm. Similar bolts had been attacking her intermittently since she was four. The past few days, though, the sensation had become especially strong. It radiated, as it always did, from the purple birthmark on her wrist, and it flowed in ripples up her arm to land deep in the pit of her stomach.

21

All Roads

Twinspeak. That was the word that came to her every single time the birthmark started to burn.

James, Louisa's fraternal twin and six minutes her junior, had worn an identical mark, his on his left wrist while Louisa's was on her right. Almost like a mirror image.

Back then, in the beginning, Louisa and James had been a rare kind of close, sharing their own private language as toddlers, dissolving into tears if there was ever an attempt to photograph them alone and not side-by-side or to dress them in anything but identically colored shirts.

In a fit of domestic rage, their father had run off with James. The two were so young—set to go to preschool together the following fall. It had been a big story, the biggest of the summer, making front-page news all through the state of Missouri; Louisa's mother still had the big bold headlines meticulously clipped in an old-fashioned scrapbook she kept under her bed. Sometimes, on the rare occasions when Louisa was house-sitting, coming over to water her mother's plants and bring in her mail, she slid it out to look at the fading print on yellowing pages: Bad divorce. Strange, conflicting stories hinting at the husband's shady personal life. Private eyes. Lakes dragged. The family car found abandoned at a bus stop. And shortly thereafter, a dead end.

Now, so many years since she'd last seen him, James had become hazy to Louisa, like an aging sunset.

And still, no official word had ever come of James's fate. The mind did horrible things when it didn't have an answer—it stretched its dark tentacles out, finding increasingly more sinister possibilities.

Finally, four years ago, on little more than a whim, her mother had tried once again to hire a private eye.

Unexpectedly, he'd come through. He'd found Louisa's father.

But the moment of elation bloomed and died in a second; Louisa's father had passed away six months earlier.

"A heart attack," the private eye'd told them— definitively, unemotionally. Charles, that was the name on his business card. Charles Mayfield, P.I., owner of Mayfield Investigations.

Mayfield was a burly man, three hundred pounds of solid muscle, with a tattoo of his daughter's name on his left forearm: *Destiny*. Louisa had stared at

23

All Roads

it, tracing the curves of the black letters as he'd report-ed his findings over coffee at their kitchen table. Louisa was still in college then—twenty years old, four full semesters under her belt.

"He used an alias," Mayfield continued. "Lived more than a decade in Oregon. Same name, same ad-dress." He flicked some pictures down on the table as he related the facts he'd gathered from friends and neighbors. A history Louisa's father seemed to have in-vented out of nowhere, like some kind of would-be novelist. A confirmed bachelor, that was what he told everyone he knew. He'd never married. Or had kids.

Those people up there in Oregon only knew Louisa's father as Greg Smith, the freewheeling guy who loved motorcycles and had a way with the ladies. They'd never seen him with a little boy.

"Why couldn't anyone else find him?" Louisa's mom had moaned, wiping her cheeks out of habit. Five, ten years earlier, they probably would have been wet. That day, they were only colorless. Ghostly. "If we'd found him alive, he could have explained. He could have told us what happened. And...*why.*"

As it was, it seemed Louisa and her mother would be left forever with questions. Where had James

24

gone? What had happened to him? Little James, with a birthmark on his wrist. Identical to his twin sister's.

She'd stared at Mayfield's tattoo until it started to blur: *Destiny.*

Louisa's wrist had burned the entire time she'd listened to her mother and Mayfield talk. But instead of flinching and trying to rub it away, she'd welcomed it. Because she had already decided she still wasn't going to accept the worst. She was going to continue to believe that the burning wrist was actually a smoldering ember of their twinspeak. It was James finding a way to tell her he was thinking of her, too.

Louisa loved this little private story, repeating it to herself as often as she could. She loved it because it let her believe that James remembered her. She loved it because it let her believe that some connections never did fade or wither.

Mostly, she loved the story because it meant that after all these years, James was still alive.

Jesse

The three of them ate to near bursting. Especially Jesse. *Home cooking,* that was what Betsy'd called it—and they were the same words Jesse would have chosen to describe the meal himself. It was like he'd been hungry for something most of his life— something he could never quite put his finger on— and suddenly, there it was, on his tongue, the taste he'd been missing all along.

The General gobbled from his bowl, consuming what must have been an entire chicken all on his own. Betsy was warm and easy to be near, but then

26

again, Jesse reminded himself, so were all his fosters when he'd first met them.

"See you in the morning," Betsy sang as Jesse stood to help gather up the Styrofoam containers.

"You mean—stay?" That couldn't be right.

"The General sure seems to think you ought to," Betsy said.

Wide-tongued and panting furiously, The General turned a few circles in front of Jesse, and dropped down into a play-bow, but for only a second. He straightened up and held his paw to shake, as though sealing the deal.

"We've kept Jesse long enough. He has places to be, surely," Louisa grumbled.

Jesse was certain that she'd hoped to rattle him with that tone of hers. Little did she know that he was used to that kind of treatment. Oh, it hadn't always been that way. In the beginning, his elementary school foster brothers had shared their bedrooms and their toys—one had even given him the top bunk—and they'd played hours of video games or sneaked out at night to ride skateboards through the neighborhood.

But the thing about being in foster care, especially as you got to be a little older, was that people

27

tended to treat you like you deserved it. Looked at you the same way they might if you were in jail. A kid who had never been adopted must have been the kind of problem that no one wanted to be permanently, legally responsible for.

The temporary sisters he'd encountered in his late adolescence had been especially distant figures. There'd been one do-gooder who had tried to introduce him to her friends at school. But most had either ignored him completely or scowled relentlessly at him over dinner tables, offering, it seemed, little more than unnecessary judgment.

Those girls helped Jesse grow quite accustomed to being spoken to in the same way Louisa just had. *Go away, go away, go away.*

This time, though, he would be more than happy to comply. In fact, the moment Betsy'd suggested spending the night, he'd immediately begun to search for signs of a decent plan to accomplish just that—a clean getaway.

"What better place to camp than right here? He's already got an RV!" Betsy swept her arm out to the side like a Price Is Right model, as though to illustrate the grandeur of their own land. The sun was

28

setting; the world was getting both oranger and colder at the same time.

"There's a trick to the back door," Betsy said.

Jesse felt his eyes swell.

"In case you need a midnight snack or to use the restroom," Betsy explained. "We've got a half-bath to the right of the kitchen."

Louisa looked on in horror as Betsy added, "It's the handle. You've got to lift up on the handle before you twist. On the back door. To get in."

"I don't think—" Louisa tried.

"Trust," Betsy barked in a whisper at Louisa, almost like a command given to The General.

Jesse tugged his sweatshirt sleeves father down his hands, swallowing up his fingers. And bit his lip, hoping the sweatshirt tug hadn't made him look dishonest.

Louisa sighed, grabbing hold of the end of her braid. "All right, then. C'mere, Gen."

But The General only plopped down at Jesse's feet.

Jesse's heart lurched. It was a sign he'd been chosen. Over Louisa.

Wasn't it? Could it really be this easy?

29

All Roads

"You've bothered that man enough, now," Louisa tried. But when she reached for The General's neck, there was no collar to tug on. She had no way of hauling him into the house.

"Why, I don't see any harm in lettin' The General and Jesse have one more boys' night together," Betsy said.

"One more—!" Louisa shouted as Betsy started dragging her toward the back door.

It was almost too perfect.

Jesse was sweating and shaking a little as he inserted the key. At ten after midnight, it felt as though the world itself was actually asleep. But nobody slept so soundly that they wouldn't wake at the roar and rattle of the old engine in his motor home coughing to life. Louisa and Betsy would come running as soon as he cranked the ignition. He'd maybe not even be off the property yet when they burst through the back door.

In the passenger seat, The General had his tongue-dangling smile going again. He began pawing at the dash as though to say, *Come on, already! Adventure awaits!*

Jesse gripped the wheel with one hand, cranked the ignition with the other, and slammed his foot onto the gas. His tires spun a bit in the damp earth, but he was moving, the house growing smaller in his rearview. When the yard sign advertising the textile shop disappeared completely, Jesse let out a whelp of victory.

He settled deep into the driver's seat, expecting relief to overtake him.

But the truth was, he already missed the place. Why? It was just a store, like any of the thousands he had stepped inside during his lifetime. The spot he'd parked was just a patch of grass and trees.

Somehow, though, it felt different to him.

Maybe it was simply that he'd been invited. He had to admit, being told he was welcome had brought some much-needed relief after years of slinking around stealthily. He'd stayed in one place only long enough to pick up a few bucks at some menial job, and had become something of an expert in picking suitable places

All Roads

(usually the edges of parks or the paved lots outside of twenty-four-hour diners or supermarkets) to furtively pull his light-blocking curtain across the windshield and catch a few hours of sleep.

He felt a little crummy for skipping out on Betsy's kind offer to spend the whole night. But then again, he reminded himself, he still had The General. And that meant he had everything he needed.

The longer he drove, though, swirling through the darkness, turning corner after corner, a new sensation began to gnaw at him, chewing away at his guts: The General didn't feel found anymore so much as stolen.

I could go back, he told himself. Drop The General off. Return him. Tie him to the porch where he couldn't get away, ring the bell, and leave.

But the instant the thought arrived, he also knew that it would never happen. He simply could not make himself turn around.

After all, Jesse had been on the road for six years, in the used RV he'd bought with the last fosters' money. And the truth was, he was lonesome. He hadn't realized how much until The General had offered his companionship.

He loved that dog. After such a short period of time—and as crazy as it sounded—he did. He loved The General for choosing him. He loved him for never being too busy to listen to him rattle on. He loved him for always being up for a new adventure, for always being so happy to see him, and for being his, in a way no other living creature had ever been before.

Mostly, he loved The General for trusting him. Wholly and unquestioningly.

Together, in his mind, he and The General had become a family.

Logically, Jesse knew that another dog would behave in much the same way. But logic rarely ever made any kind of impact on a man's heart.

And so he drove on, forging ahead, refusing to turn back.

The roads here didn't just curve; they spiraled. The map stretched across his dash offered no help. He couldn't quite figure out where they were, exactly. Some spec too small to have made it to the page. Perhaps, he reasoned, they were twisting around one of those infamous Ozark Mountains. As soon as they hit the base of this particular hill, the road would surely straighten out.

All Roads

The awful guilty feeling of taking The General would quiet down over time, he assured himself.

His tires slumped into a patch of journey-ending mud before the sun had finished rising. Jesse cursed quietly under his breath.

The General jumped from the passenger seat and launched himself against the door hard enough to jar it open.

"General!" Jesse gasped as he lunged outside, too.

Instead of making a run for it, galloping off like he had at the very beginning of this whole crazy mess, The General stopped just outside the door, and began barking and jumping and turning in circles.

"What're you so excited—?" Jesse stopped abruptly, one foot dangling out the doorway when he saw her—the baggy jeans, the mess of a braid. Louisa. Stooping to rub The General's ears.

"Where—?" he tried.

Looming behind Louisa, the house and field he'd left last night provided the answer.

Jesse was right back where he started.

"Breakfast?" Betsy asked as she brought him a cup of black coffee, a sunny-side-up smile on her face.

Louisa

"**O**ne thing's for sure. That guy tried to take off last night." Louisa offered up her hands, palm out, for emphasis.

Her longtime boyfriend, Sean, only hurried on ahead of her. He was still wearing his ugliest boots, a black rubber pair that looked more like fireman's boots, the ones he always put on to hit the fields shortly after dawn. Somehow, it was easier for her to look at the boots than the back of his head. The tools inside his gray handled chest with the rusted corners rattled with nearly every step. Could he even hear her over that racket?

"I woke up this morning, Sean, and I heard his engine running," Louisa said, louder now. "His *engine,* even though Betsy invited him to stay the night. Even though he was supposed to be camping out behind the house. Running his generator, give me a break. And get this—he was parked facing the opposite direction this morning. How much more obvious do you have to be?"

In the distance, The General raced happily toward a patch of dirt. He paused, taking the time to find just the right spot before he began to dig furiously, throwing dirt everywhere. He loved to dig. *Obsessed*—that was a good word for it. Louisa had often thought that half of the wildflowers in the area had been spread by The General himself. He'd collected pollen and seeds in his fur and paws and tracked them everywhere, depositing it all in the ground he tilled with his toenails. Kind of like a four-legged Johnny Appleseed, but for Queen Anne's lace and red clover.

The General finished his hole quickly and galloped toward the herd of grass-fed Black Angus that was at the heart of Sean's family business. Handed down from parent to child for the last five generations.

Now that's a real family, Louisa thought, twisting to glance over her shoulder toward the ancient white farmhouse. Yes, five generations and counting, roots as thick as the body of the 1942 Chevrolet pickup Sean had rebuilt, the one his great-grandfather had driven. His strong family ties were maybe what had drawn her to Sean in the first place—even more than his sturdy, rugged farm boy good looks.

"The worst part is, he had The General in his RV the whole time. I swear, he's up to something. I had an awful feeling that he would try to steal The General last night. But Betsy—"

"Come on, Lou. Took off and came back?" A wayward lock of black hair tumbled toward his eyebrow as he shook his head. "It doesn't make sense. If he wanted to leave with The General, why not—you know—leave with The General? Why come back?"

"That's exactly what I mean! It's about more than my dog now. It has to be, right?"

Sean put his tool chest on the ground and reached for the broken gate with only a twisted wire holding it shut.

A repair job. While his brother's tractor hummed in the distance. They were still able to hay

37

All Roads

here in the last days of November, thanks to the unusual lingering warmth. The General galloped closer to the tractor, barking now. Angry barking, accompanied by jumping and lunging. So worked up, white foamy spit was probably collecting around the edges of his mouth. But it wasn't the tractor The General was barking at. It was Sean's brother, Luke, who was regularly the recipient of bared teeth and growling. Not that anyone understood why. Not when The General was usually so loving and friendly.

Louisa stuck her hands in her pockets and waited for Sean to say something else. But he was squinting at the gate in a way that told her his thoughts had drifted away from her story. Couldn't he see that Louisa's situation needing fixing, too?

"This morning, Betsy sent him out for a *pumpkin*," Louisa insisted.

Sean burst out in a hearty laugh. The kind that burned and scraped. Sometimes, laughter was like that. Sometimes it attacked, leaving welts behind, just like the stinging nettles that often hid in the area's gardens and along fence rows.

"It's not a joke," Louisa insisted. "She told him all about our big Thanksgiving dinner. And then she sent him out to get a pumpkin for the pie. *Our* pie. A complete stranger."

"I know your grandmother pretty well," Sean reminded Louisa.

She rocked back on her heels. Somehow, it was hard to think of it that way—of someone outside the family possibly knowing her grandmother as well as she did. Better, even. But it was true; he was right.

Sean had grown up so close—practically in Betsy's backyard—and Louisa had grown up a few miles away, never really bothering to get to know her grandmother as a person until she had gotten interested in Betsy's occupation. (Actually, *obsessed* was still a better word—she'd gotten just as obsessed with the fiber arts as The General was with digging.) Even now, two full years after joining forces as business partners, two years after it had become clear that their long work hours meant it was only practical for them to share a living space, splitting the bills and the chores and even taking turns walking The General 50/50, the two women were still getting to know each other as individuals.

After a full quarter century of paying attention, though, Sean seemed to have Louisa's grandmother all figured out.

39

All Roads

"If Betsy says he's good people, then he's good people," Sean insisted, unwinding the wire from the gate.

"That's a lovely sentiment," Louisa muttered.

"But you don't believe her."

"Believe that she could accurately size a person up after spending thirty seconds with him on the sidewalk outside of Katy's Kitchen? Sorry."

"The General went with him, though. Right? I know The General, too. He's a good dog, but he's got definite opinions."

Sean straightened up, nodded once toward the tractor his brother was using in the nearby field. The General was still barking furiously. Frustrated, Luke had started shouting back. Something along the lines of, "*Git, git.*" He snatched off his ball cap and started waving it for emphasis. "Scat!" The General only persisted, lowering his head in a way that warned he was about to take that tractor down. And Luke—the obvious enemy—would go down with it.

"Look at him out there. You really think that dog would go along with anybody he didn't have one hundred percent total confidence in?"

"Hunger keeps any creature from thinking

straight."

"In the first place, do you even know when Jesse and The General crossed paths? Huh? Day what? Day three, day four? Day one? Besides, he couldn't have been too hungry the day he met that Jesse person. No matter how long he'd been on the loose when they crossed paths. That dog's a hunter. I know all about those 'presents' he brings you. The two of us have been laughing about that since the first day The General ever went for a hunt. The way he carries his kills to the back of the house, always dropping them by something of yours—your shoes or the jacket you left in a lawn chair. He could have lived forever on rabbit or squirrel or blue jay. Saw him with a hawk in his mouth once. Hand to God. The General chose that guy. Jesse. And not because he was on the brink of starvation."

The mere mention of eating brought the morning's breakfast to Louisa's mind. How Betsy and Jesse had passed sections of the newspaper across the kitchen table as though the scene was perfectly normal. How The General had gobbled his own eggs before resting his chin on the toe of Jesse's gray, cracked sneaker. Louisa, meanwhile, had kept her eye on Jesse as he'd eaten his scrambled eggs, searching for some

41

All Roads

clue in his face. Some sign as to what this was all about. She'd felt that they were being played for fools. But to what end? What was Jesse after?

What's wrong with you? she'd wanted to scream at Betsy and The General.

Now, in front of Sean, she wanted to scream it again.

Louisa sighed. "He's back, though." It was all she could manage. Cats came back after you fed them. Boys came back after you kissed them. What tidbit—other than maybe a taste of hospitality—had they offered this Jesse guy? What was bringing him back? What did he want?

"Yep," Sean agreed, reaching for an ancient Chase & Sanborn coffee can filled with random sized screws, "The General's back, all right. Man, it was good to see him this morning. I can't imagine how it must've felt when you saw him."

"No," Louisa said, stuffing her hands in her pockets. "*Him* him. Jesse."

Sean paused, glancing up at her through another wayward black lock that had tumbled down his forehead.

Always before, she had pitched right in and

42

helped when she'd shown up to find him in the middle of some farm project. Women who refused to get their fingers dirty made her cringe. She was able-bodied, the same as Sean, and maybe even more so than semi-useless Luke, who half the time was popping some sort of over-the-counter pill that offered little help with his current hangover. She had learned to drive his family tractor and had helped spread grass seed in feeding pastures and shear the sheep (of course she'd helped shear the sheep—buying raw wool for her spinning was how she'd met Sean in the first place), and she had never once come over and simply hovered over him, like she was too dainty for hammers and nails.

Now, though, she wasn't even taking that coffee can from him, helping him find the right size screw. Now, the questioned begged: What was wrong with *her*?

"Never seen you so suspicious before," Sean observed. The tone in his voice—it was disappointment. It sounded worse to her, even, than the disappointment Betsy'd expressed the night before.

In the distance, The General continued to bark. And growl. And chase a tractor far too big to ever be taken down by any single living creature.

All Roads

*A*fter loading her pickup—the same old '75 GMC she and Betsy took turns driving to town—with another load of Sean's wool, Louisa poured a bowl of water from her thermos for a frantically panting General. She gave him a few minutes to recuperate, leaving him to lie on his elbows in the cool shade. When his tongue finally started to shrink, no longer looking even wider than his skull, Louisa whistled, calling him into the cab.

Sean leaned in through the rolled-down window to kiss her goodbye. "Remember—even if you don't want to trust anybody else, you can always trust The General." He patted the truck door for emphasis and turned back toward the never-ending list of errands that always awaited a farmer.

Louisa took off, The General sitting beside her, his face pointed toward the windshield, eyes fixed on the road before him. She kept him in her peripheral vision until the first stoplight, when she turned to him and asked, "What's the deal with this Jesse guy? You spent all that time with him. What gives?"

The General cocked his head. His tongue rolled to the side of his mouth. He merely panted in response.

"Some help you are," Louisa grumbled as she rubbed behind his ear.

The General leaned into her hand and thumped the seat with his back foot.

Louisa sucked in a single sharp inhale when the all-too-familiar lightning bolt of pain hit. Her birthmark was stinging again. Like she was being attacked by a whole hive full of bees. She grabbed her wrist, squeezing and hoping for the searing agony to die down.

The car behind her honked—two short annoyed beeps. Louisa glanced up, away from her wrist. She hadn't noticed the light turning green.

"Okay, okay," Louisa muttered. She pressed against the gas and steered through the intersection. But instead of heading straight back to Betsy's, Louisa took a detour.

"You and I have to make a stop first," she told

All Roads

The General.

The county library was still housed, as it had been for more than forty years, in a tiny redbrick building a stone's throw from the square. Though from the outside the library promised to be less than impressive, in truth, it boasted one of the best collections of historical fiction in the state as well as a sprawling computer lab.

Louisa knocked on the back door. It opened, and a young man filled the space with his slender frame. He coughed, adjusted his glasses, stuck his hands in his pockets. "Hey, Louisa," he said, offering a crooked smile.

"We just need ten minutes," Louisa said.

"We?" His eyes darted toward The General, panting at Louisa's side.

Louisa grinned and patted her leg, summoning The General as she took a step toward the open door.

Robert, the seventeen-year-old who manned the computer lab through his high school's work study program, let out only the tiniest hiccup of protest. He was intimidated by her—Louisa knew that. Betsy had occasionally volunteered a teenage Louisa to be his babysitter while she was visiting; as a result, she had some pretty good dirt on his younger years. Besides, it was kind of hard for anyone to redefine a person they had branded, at the very beginning, as an authority figure. Even now, Louisa bet he would click his lights off if she told him it was bedtime.

He fidgeted as Louisa and The General stepped inside. At midmorning on a Tuesday, the lab was characteristically empty. She and The General would leave before anyone even knew they were there.

She knew she could do her searches for James at home and not bother Robert at all. But she didn't want Betsy to know what she was doing. After Mayfield's kitchen-table revelation, there had been a kind of sad acceptance shared between Louisa's mother and grandmother. Enough. They'd had enough. Best for her to look for her brother in relative private.

Louisa settled into a terminal close to the back door. The General sat beside her, his soft pant like the

All Roads

tick of a second hand.

She tried Googling James. Looking for him on Facebook. She ran a simple people search. She tried White Pages. It seemed a little ridiculous to be looking up his real name. But what else did she have? She even tried Greg Smith, James Smith. But that last name was so painfully common—surely why her father had chosen it to begin with.

She Googled her mother's name and James's together. And was greeted by a long string of articles from that awful summer. His disappearance. All information she had seen before.

After a while, it wasn't entirely clear what she was hunting for anymore. She typed Jesse's name in with The General's on Facebook and Twitter, but what did she think that would get her? Some sort of "Found Dog" post? What good would that do? What proof would it offer?

Robert offered a fake cough. Louisa raised her head; her ten minutes had passed by five minutes ago. The adult and children's services librarians were chattering beyond the lab's door.

She logged out; all she was doing was traveling in circles around dead ends, anyway.

48

As she stood and patted her leg, wordlessly asking The General to follow, her mind exploded with familiar questions.

Did James even remember that he had a twin sister with an identical birthmark on her wrist?

And was the fact that she was thinking of him making his own wrist burn and itch and tingle?

Betsy

*N*ever before had Betsy been so grateful that it was Louisa's day to pick up a load of wool from Sean.

In fact, the moment Louisa'd pulled out of her parking space, Betsy'd immediately attacked her phone. And she'd called her daughter.

"Katy," Betsy barked. "Can you still get in touch with that last investigator?"

"I think so," Katy said, caution drawing out her words. "Why?"

Betsy sucked in a breath as she lowered herself onto the corner of her desk. She glanced through the front window, grateful no customer had slipped through the door yet. Actually, she doubted any would slip through this close to Thanksgiving. Business always dried up completely right before the annual family feast, then exploded come Small Business Saturday.

She shook her head at herself. How could she be thinking of holiday sales?

Because it's easier than telling Katy what's actually been on your mind, she reminded herself.

"Mom?" Katy asked. The usual diner sounds at Katy's Kitchen clattered in the background. "Mom? Why do you need an investigator?"

"We," Betsy corrected. "We need one."

"Something hasn't happened, has it?" Katy's gasp rattled through the phone, attacking Betsy's ear. "Louisa—"

"No, no," Betsy insisted. "Louisa's fine. We have a visitor. Brought back The General."

"Yes! The General!" Katy shouted. "I was so glad to see him yesterday when you knocked on the diner window. Louisa must be so relieved."

"Katy, the man who brought him—you saw him, too, right?"

All Roads

"Yeah. Kind of. I was mostly focused on The General. Why?"

"He's still here."

"He is."

Betsy could tell that Katy had stepped away from the more high-traffic areas of the diner. Background noises had all but disappeared completely. Katy was expecting to need some privacy.

Would knowing Katy was now mostly alone, where she could collapse or cry or shake if she needed, make delivering this news any easier? Of course not. Nothing about this had been easy. The shock of it all had shaken Betsy's core, but it was still her daughter who had suffered the most.

Poor Katy. It was as if, twenty years ago, someone had inserted an instrument of torture deep into her soul—one that could never again be removed—and every single time she'd checked out a tip or a new lead, every single time she'd begun to think that finally, an answer might come, she'd only wound up twisting it in a little deeper.

"What does it mean?" Katy asked. "Mom? What does it mean that he's still here?"

"He—is the same age as Louisa. Roughly."

"Yes?"

"And…" Betsy rubbed her sweaty forehead. Sturdy and healthy, she had never been one to focus on age. But opening her daughter up to yet another *maybe*, another *it's possible*, another *what-if* was making her feel every last second of her sixty-eight years.

"He's the same height as Louisa, too," Betsy finally added.

"*And?*"

"His last name is Smith. Goes by Jesse."

"Jesse?" Katy's voice was high-pitched now. Almost screechy. "We used to know a James who went by Jesse. Remember? A nickname. And Smith—just like—that alias his father picked in Oregon…"

Betsy cringed. She wished she'd hired a private eye herself. But that last P.I.—he was already familiar with this case. He'd found Katy's husband. Sometimes, having had a little success made a person work harder. Faster. She would need that kind of speed. Answers before Jesse took off.

"Anything else?" Katy begged.

There was, actually. Betsy had seen it with her own eyes—proof. But if she mentioned it, what she'd seen, it would bring back the possibility of a happy

53

ending. Not just a faintly renewed glimmer of a *could-be*, either, but the kind of fresh, powerful *it's all going to be okay* they'd all had at the very beginning. When they'd felt certain they would be with James again... and quickly.

Betsy couldn't do that to Katy. So she steered around the proof and offered instead, "He—has a tic. An eye tic."

Silence.

"So did James," Katy whispered. "Did Louisa see it?" Her voice cracked as she mentioned her own daughter.

"I don't think so. She's not quite seeing straight. She's got it in her head that he wants to keep The General for himself."

Silence.

"Smith is such a common name," Katy lamented.

"I also have his license plate number," Betsy said. "I was hoping that P.I. of yours could use it to trace him back. Find out where he came from."

Silence.

"Still. Could be another scam," Katy muttered.

"Yes."

54

"You and I, we went through a lot of those."

"Yes."

"Scams Louisa doesn't even know about."

"Yes."

"Pay me upfront, and I'll get you great results. I'll find your kid," Katy recited bitterly. "And this guy—Jesse—he's wiggling himself into your good graces. Showing himself to be trustworthy. Taking care of The General. But the question is did The General really go missing, or did this guy take him, keep him a few days, and then bring him back, right when we were feeling like all was lost? I mean, a quick Google would tell him everything about what we'd been through. He could use that to his advantage, wreak a little psychological warfare, just like all the rest of the scam artists did."

"That's right."

"And even though we kept those scams hidden from Louisa back when she was little, even though she's not really that aware of what kind of problems we've had with this stuff in the past, she's already got a bad feeling about this guy."

Betsy sighed. "Yes." She was getting woozy. Why had she brought it up at all? Now she was even beginning to doubt that what she'd seen really amounted to proof. She was glad she hadn't mentioned it.

Silence swelled yet again.

And in that silence, even though both of the women knew better—even though their experience had taught them that they should be expecting this man to turn out to be desperate and cruel, a vulture feeding off the carcasses of dead hopes—Betsy felt the tension on the line begin to change. And she knew they were both thinking the same thing: *It could also be the miracle we've all wished for.*

"Can you get him to stay a little longer?" Katy asked. "Long enough for the investigator to track something down on him?"

"I was thinking the same thing—that he'd need to stay—so I gave him a job. Not a big one, but I told him I hadn't had time to get my pie ingredients. Been too busy. I always use a fresh pumpkin, you know that. Can't stand that canned stuff. I thought if I based my story on the truth, he'd be more likely to believe me. But, yes. I think I can do something along the same lines to keep him around tomorrow. Some other job to make him stay."

"I'm calling that private eye right now. His

number's still in my phone," Katy declared, and then the line went dead.

All Roads

Jesse

*N*o matter how hard he tried, Jesse could not find a single explanation that seemed to fit. Alone in his RV, driving and driving with the goal of finding the perfect pumpkin for Betsy's pie, he had plenty of time to relive the night before. To figure out how he could have possibly set out in one direction only to wind up in the exact same place he'd started.

It only felt like you were heading in a straight line because you didn't come to an intersection, he finally told himself. *You actually traveled in a circle. Winding around and around back to where you started.*

58

And then he waited to see if this grabbed-out-of-thin-air explanation rubbed against him in an uncomfortable way, indicating it couldn't possibly be the right solution, either.

Actually, it didn't seem too far off. Hadn't there been a man at the gas station who had tried to warn him about such a thing? Hadn't the guy still been rattling on about the treacherous winding Ozark Mountains when The General had bolted from the window?

Yes—it sort of made sense, actually.

But, no; then again, it didn't account for the strange feeling that had accompanied him as he'd driven through the night. Kind of like a tug—a magnetic force—pulling him back toward the open field behind Betsy's house, where The General had galloped off, looking achingly free.

Couldn't Jesse feel every bit as free there? He didn't really have to leave, he reasoned. He could stay, maybe find a permanent place nearby...

But then what? Share The General with Louisa? Come and visit him every so often? That would never work. The General would have his own family, one that Jesse would never completely be allowed into. It would hurt too much to be near his dog but know he officially belonged to someone else.

No, Jesse would definitely have to go. And The General would definitely have to go with him.

At least he'd wormed his way into another shot at a breakout. He could make his pumpkin-buying errand drag on until the evening. Of course he could. And once he returned, there would be another dinner, another *You couldn't possibly take off now, so late in the day*. Another camp-out behind Betsy's house with The General. Another wait-for-the-house-lights-to-go-off start of the engine. This time, he wouldn't get turned around or confused. This time, he'd get out of town.

The mere fact that he was capable of forging a black-hearted, rotten plan to steal the dog Louisa seemed to love as much as he did made him feel sick to his stomach.

But he also knew he would never be able to leave the only creature who had ever shown him genuine affection.

No. Not literally the only, he corrected himself. And cringed. He wasn't even sure the other one counted. He'd been such a little kid. His memory of that time was fuzzy, and he wasn't quite sure if the person he remembered was a biological parent or just an early foster.

Jesse'd overheard one social worker telling another years ago that his records were incomplete. How could that have possibly happened? They didn't seem to know. A computer glitch, maybe. A coffee spill on a keyboard. Something small and utterly ridiculous. And *poof*—with not a single individual in his life who personally knew where he'd come from, his history had been erased. So much of his own life remained a mystery to him.

As he grew older, he hadn't pressed it, asked anyone else or done a records search of his own. He figured it wasn't worth tracking down, anyway, the tale of how he'd become a foster kid. It was probably something as hurtful as no one wanting him. Who wanted to come face-to-face with that? He was also halfway afraid that his early memory of affection was fuzzy because he'd purposefully made it so, to block something out that was bad. Best not to disturb the giant rock sometimes—especially when you were sure that all that was under there was a bunch of snakes.

The Winnebago jostled down a dirt road as he scanned the acres for signs of a cornfield. The kind of place that last month would have been used as a Hal-

All Roads

loween maze populated with zombies jumping out at costumed kids. The kind of place that would have sold pumpkins for jack-o'-lanterns. The kind that would still maybe have a pumpkin left for Betsy's pie.

He wasn't sure, really, why it was so important to him to please Betsy. Or why she'd wanted him to stick around—but she did, didn't she? Why else would she come up with a job for him, and a pretty lame one at that? His eyes darted about, but the landscape was the kind of monotonous that let his mind continue to travel, meandering down one path and up another.

It occurred to him that it was the first time in two weeks he didn't have The General at his side, and it gave him a terrible ache. Like Jesse was missing an arm or a leg, something he wasn't quite sure how to function without. Phantom pains. Wasn't that what you called it when something that belonged to you was severed?

He sighed, beginning to wonder if he'd ever find an actual pumpkin patch.

As he puttered along, the RV made him feel like a turtle, carrying his shell around everywhere he went. The slowness of the drive only emphasized it.

At least, until a cardboard sign flapped onto

62

his windshield, blocking his view. Then the turtle-like crawl came to a gravel-spraying halt.

He idled there in the road, with the weathered cardboard plastered against the glass. A hand-painted "Pumpkin Patch" and an arrow hovered right in front of his face.

Jesse popped the driver-side door and stepped out, tugging the cardboard away. A couple strips of silver duct tape still attached to the sign's edges kept sticking to the side of the RV as he tried to slide it free.

On the opposite side of the road, a small metal flag stake pointed toward a nearby narrow dirt lane. A piece of silver duct tape rippled from the stake in the autumn wind.

Strangely, Jesse felt it again: a tug. Just as he'd felt the night before. He folded the sign and climbed behind the steering wheel, tossed the cardboard into the passenger seat.

He traveled the length of the dirt path, bumping along, swerving to avoid both a low tree branch and a pile of rocks that had been washed into the lane, perhaps by some of the recent heavy rains.

Another sign—this one wooden and branded, "Griffey Family Farms"—brought his foot to the

63

brake again.

"Been waitin' on you," an older man shouted, before Jesse had even completely pulled himself from his RV. He wore torn denim coveralls, a stained red flannel shirt, and a faded baseball cap advertising a feed and grain store, the kind with the plastic mesh back.

"Come on, come on," the man urged.

Jesse followed as the man rocked back and forth, limping through the mud toward a sprawling field of pumpkins. Glistening pumpkins. Kissed by dew pumpkins—even now, easing toward late morning.

"So many—" Jesse sighed.

"Yes!" the man shouted. "Unexpected yield this year. Right in time for Thanksgiving. Why I hired all you extra hands to help with the picking."

"Oh, I—"

The man raised a bushy gray eyebrow. Rather than mere wrinkles, he had regular garden rows in his face. "Yes?"

But the patch was strangely inviting, and Jesse had hours to fill before heading back to Betsy's. He was used to this kind of work, too. Maybe, at this point, he even had a kind of day-laborer look about him. Besides, the way that man was eyeing him made Jesse want to lend a hand. Inexplicably. So Jesse smiled and said, "Nothing—just—point me in the right direction."

The man handed him a pair of pruners.

"How—?" Jesse called out. He opened and shut the pruners a couple of times, fast enough to make a slicing sound, embarrassed to finish his question.

The old man sighed. "Make sure to choose firm ones. With good color. And leave four inches or so on the stem. Keeps better. Not that it has to keep for very long. Got a local grocer comin' to pick up just 'bout the whole lot of 'em later today."

Jesse set to work, joining others already in the field. As he cut and hauled the pumpkins to a flatbed trailer, he swore he heard the sound of children. Two of them. Laughing and chasing each other. Their giggles intertwined, like vines.

But when he looked, he saw no one. Which was odd. They'd sounded so close.

Maybe, he thought, his mind was telling stories. He'd come up with some wild ones these last few years, tales that he used when he pulled into a new town and introduced himself, tales that offered some

65

All Roads

better-sounding reasons for being on the road and looking for work for the day. Honorable stories, mostly about trying to get to a family that was waiting on him. Sometimes, in addition to work, his tales occasionally made someone feel sorry enough that they offered him Wi-Fi access or a free night's stay in a real RV park, the kind of place where he wouldn't have to pull the privacy curtain across his windshield, concealing the sleeping passenger inside.

He had become quite good at his storytelling, embellishing here and there, but never overdoing it to the point that people began to wrinkle their foreheads in a quizzical way.

He even told his stories to himself, at times, when no one was around.

He'd begun to wonder if you could tell a story to yourself so many times that you believed it. Or if you could tell yourself a story so many times that you began to believe you were a different kind of person. A better one. The kind who would never have to tell such stories to begin with.

He worked until the old man approached him with his pay. Jesse waved him away. "Just came for a pumpkin. You give me one of your best, we'll call it

66

even."

"You mean you're not a hired hand?"

"No."

He wheezed a laugh. "What'd you do all that work for?"

"You needed it."

The old man cocked his head. "Huh," he said. "Only people I ever had just pitch in like that were my sons. And my grandniece."

Jesse shrugged as he started toward the pumpkin he'd had his eye on, one he'd set aside from the others, beneath the shade of an oak tree by the man's house.

"What you got planned, son?" the man called out.

"Planned?" The only plan he had was the one to steal The General. How could the man possibly know that?

"No fellow as young as yourself just up and buys himself a pumpkin without a plan behind it."

"Oh," Jesse sighed, relaxing. "It's for someone else. Betsy."

"Betsy! Stitch in Time Betsy? From the store?"

"You know her?"

All Roads

"Know her!" the man shouted. "She's my sister."

Can the world really truly be this small? Jesse wondered as he shook the man's hand and they finally introduced themselves, exchanging names. Tom—Betsy's brother's name was Tom. For some reason that Jesse couldn't quite pinpoint, it felt good knowing that.

"How'd you meet?" Tom asked.

"I—brought—The General."

"He's back!" Tom exclaimed. "What a relief. That poor Louisa. She doesn't take to losing things too well."

"She doesn't."

"No. She lost—well. It's a long story. We all lose things we love, but when you lose something important to you at such a young age..."

"Yes," Jesse agreed, even though he had no idea what Tom was talking about.

"She sure does love pumpkin pie, though," Tom went on. "That Louisa. I remember, when she was little, she'd be at Thanksgiving dinner with it smeared across her whole face. In her hair. All over her dress."

Again, Jesse swore he heard giggles. Children just had to be nearby, didn't they? Only, when he

68

glanced over his shoulder—still no sign of a single child anywhere.

"Grab two, son, grab two. For Betsy. I owe you a lot more than that."

Jesse nodded, waving off another offer of money.

"How 'bout you? You like a good pumpkin pie?"

"I don't know. I guess."

"You guess?"

"I've had a lot of bad pies." It was true, actually. Being a foster mother didn't necessarily mean you had any command over the kitchen.

Tom slapped his arm. "Your luck is about to change, young man." He winked, and as he turned, he shouted, "See you at Thanksgiving!"

"See, I'm not—" Jesse tried, because he would no more be invited to their Thanksgiving than he would be invited to a stranger's wedding. But Tom was already swaying back and forth in another direction, limping and waving at an approaching grocery truck.

Halfway back to Betsy's place, the previous night of driving and the full day of work in Tom's pumpkin patch caught up to him. Overwhelmed by

69

All Roads

pure exhaustion, Jesse pulled over, into a field. He parked beneath a tree and slept, his ears still filled with the familiar echoes of children's laughter.

Hours later, he pulled back into a parking space outside the textile shop, the kind marked off by white lines and intended for temporary visitors. No way could he be presumptuous enough to pull into the driveway, let alone around to the back of the house, where he'd started the night before. He needed permission first.

Louisa's truck was back, he noted as he tugged his pumpkins from his RV, one in each arm.

As soon as he entered A Stitch in Time, The General jumped up on him, putting his paws on his waist and barking excitedly.

Betsy was jumping to her feet, too, shouting, "Look at those amazing pumpkins! Where'd you find them?" Which was followed closely by, "Did you have to drive far? So much effort for our one ingredient! Have you eaten? Are you hungry?"

And it seemed to Jesse that for once, he had two creatures glad to see him return. An honest smile spread across his cheeks.

"Well, Tom's were so perfect, who could pick one?" he shouted at Betsy over The General's inces-

70

sant barking.

"Tom!" Betsy clapped her hands a couple of times and laughed.

In the background, Louisa scowled. "I didn't know you sent him to Tom's place."

"No—he *found* Tom," Betsy corrected. And smiled, pleased.

They ate beneath the dogwoods again, another picnic. This time, navy beans and homemade cornbread. Jesse complimented Betsy. "Every bit as good as the meal from the night before. Better, even," he corrected himself, his words muffled by mouthfuls of food.

"You should be here after Louisa goes fishing," Betsy announced. "Best angler around. Now, *that's* a good meal."

Louisa flinched.

Dinner went on—passing bowls, taking seconds...then thirds. Finishing up with coffee and fresh rhubarb pie. His conversation with Betsy reminded Jesse of the roads from the night before, winding and arriving nowhere new, circling back to the same starting point. This time, the familiar starting spot was Betsy's invitation to stay the night.

71

All Roads

*U*nder the stars, Jesse crept toward the house, blowing his dog whistle all the way. Blowing and blowing and feeling grateful that Louisa'd obviously had no idea he had such a whistle when she'd brought The General in to spend the night with her. He lifted the handle on the back door, and out jumped an excited General.

"Shhh," Jesse chastised, ushering him into the Winnebago.

Once they were both settled in their seats and The General was wearing his ready-for-adventure tongue-dangling grin, Jesse asked, "What if I told you we were going to leave for good? Would you be less enthusiastic?"

The General only yipped.

"I mean it. That's how these things go with me. A short stay, and then you're supposed to move on." *Foster kid.* Even now.

Again, a yip. *Get to it.*

Jesse started the engine. This time, he paid special attention to where he was going. He tried to remember the specific turns he'd taken the night before, and always chose to swerve in the opposite direction. As he drove, he thought about Tom. He thought about being in the same place long enough to watch a seed grow into a tiny sprout, then into a plant full of lush blooming flowers. He thought about seeing the same faces every day. He thought about having no blanks in your history.

His wandering mind made him lose track of where he was, exactly. But when the tug found him again, he sighed with relief. That tug would help lead him where he most wanted to go. Of course it would. That tug was nothing more than his gut instinct telling him how to cross out of the city limits.

That was right, wasn't it? Where he most wanted to be was away, out of town.

Except...

Finding The General, finding Tom, the sign flapping onto his windshield, the sound of children coming to him when there were none. What was this place? How could there be so many strange happenings and coincidences?

Jesse shook his head at himself. Why was he reading so much into all this? It wasn't so magical or unusual to like the feel of such a rural place. What person didn't feel instantly at home under an unpolluted sky, stiff autumn grass like a new front door welcome mat beneath your feet? That was all.

And the laughter? It'd simply been a daydream. His mind continuing to tell wild tales. Even though he knew better, he'd been fantasizing about staying. If he didn't watch it, before long, he'd be trying to convince himself he was a wildflower, with roots literally stuck beneath the soil. That he'd die if he tried to uproot himself.

How ridiculous. Jesse was wheels, not roots. He would be, most likely, for the rest of his life.

Just as the sun started to rise—and he was about to breathe a sigh of relief—The General jumped from the passenger seat and began to whine.

"What is it, boy?" Jesse asked, putting the RV in park.

The General continued to bark and yip and whimper, pawing at the door.

"You need to go out?" Jesse asked.

He paused, his fingers on the door handle. Where did he hope they were?

All roads lead to home. That was what Betsy'd said at the very beginning.

Yes. That was right. The roads had led him to the next town over. That was his home. His and The General's. For today, anyway.

When he twisted the door handle, The General launched himself outside.

"Morning," Betsy called out, pushing a coffee cup toward him.

All Roads

Louisa

This was getting scary. Betsy asked Jesse to get a pumpkin and he just happened to wind up at her brother's place? How was that possible? Did he already know who Tom was before he headed out?

Why wasn't Betsy taking this seriously?

"Seems I have another night to settle up for," Jesse said over breakfast. Their second breakfast together. He sounded so ridiculously perky.

Louisa grimaced. It was easy to be in a bad mood this morning, what with her wrist burning like it was. It had never been this bad before. If Betsy had paid less attention to Jesse and more to her, she would have realized that Louisa had spent the entirety of breakfast with her wrist pressed against her orange juice glass, soaking up the cool comfort.

"Nothing to settle," Louisa said emphatically. "You brought The General back. No amount of hospitality on our end could ever repay you. So..." She nodded at him once, her wild, yet-to-be-braided hair falling in front of her eyes. But it was the tone of her voice that finished the sentence: ...*it's way past time for you to go.*

Betsy ignored her, gathering their plates as she announced, sweetly, "I'd love some fresh cloves. For the pie."

Louisa's frown deepened. Another silly errand. Rather than arguing with her grandmother, she slammed her chair under the table and shouted, "Deliveries," even though she didn't have any yet to make. She hurried past the wool she'd picked up from Sean yesterday while reminding herself she really needed to stop messing around and get to work spinning. It would soon be Small Business Saturday, and women bought a ton of yarn once it turned cold. Knitting really was a wintertime occupation. Nobody sat poolside

77

making mufflers, after all.

But she made a big deal of putting The General in the passenger seat, starting the engine, and then, to stall just a little bit longer, rifling through her glove compartment. From the corner of her eye, she watched as Jesse climbed into his RV.

She pulled out a few seconds after he did, and she began to follow the Winnebago, her heart thumping in every part of her body—and that crazy birthmark of hers buzzing in syncopated response.

"Did something happen last night?" Louisa asked The General. "Your fur was cold when I first pet you this morning. Who let you out? And when? You were supposed to spend the whole night in my room. Where were you really?"

The General pawed at the window. Louisa sighed and rolled it down.

Her dog's would-be thief steered onto the highway, sticking his arm out the window, mimicking an airplane. From somewhere under the section of her brain reserved for scenes that had played out long ago, Louisa suddenly remembered a little boy doing the same thing, humming with his lips pressed together to make an engine sound. Who had it been? A friend? One of her long-ago classmates, a neighbor her mother had driven to school? Most likely. Right then, though, for some reason (maybe the ache in her wrist), Louisa wanted it to be a foggy memory of James.

Jesse's brake lights flashed. Did he know she was trailing him? Was he about to take her on some ridiculous goose chase? Was he messing with her mind?

Louisa glared at the Winnebago.

In the back of her mind, she still heard Sean's surprised voice. *Never seen you so suspicious before.* Sometimes, though, suspiciousness wasn't a symptom of paranoia. Sometimes, it was plain right.

What grown man acted like a stray dog, pawing at somebody's back door, begging to be taken in?

She tightened her grip on the steering wheel as she strengthened her resolve. She followed the Winnebago at a safe distance down the highway, then clicked her own turn signal when he drifted toward an off-ramp. They coasted into a nearby small town. The same town, Louisa thought uncomfortably, where she had lost The General while delivering her goods to a craft supplies store.

They meandered toward the business district. It was hard figuring out how to stay back but not lose

79

All Roads

Jesse. She hoped that the tiny back window of the Winnebago—which she figured had to be the bathroom window—was hard to see through using his rearview mirror.

She was so focused on her following technique, she didn't quite realize exactly where they were headed.

Until he stopped.

Outside a florist shop.

She flopped back against the bench seat, mouth agape. "How is this possible?" she asked The General.

Here Jesse was again, heading for another run-in with another member of her family. Flowers by Esther, owned by Louisa's cousin. But the weirdest part of all—the part that was making the hair literally stand up on the back of her neck—was that this particular cousin also happened to sell spices that came from flowers: real vanilla, for example, that came from orchids.

And cloves. The woman sold cloves.

How could Jesse know that?

Louisa's mouth was dry, her head throbbing, and her wrist burned like she was being branded when Jesse emerged from the store with a shopping bag—surely containing the cloves he had set out to get—and

80

a pot of mums.

Betsy loved mums. Especially the purple ones. Just like the ones he was carrying.

*B*ack home, Louisa confronted Betsy, "Tell the truth. Don't you think this is a bit too coincidental? Tom *and* Esther?"

"Is that what you were doing today?" Betsy asked. "Instead of making deliveries, you were what? Spying on him?"

"Shouldn't somebody at this point?"

"Think about this whole thing from his perspective," Betsy insisted. "It's got to seem to him that every single business and plot of land in town is owned by some member of our family."

"That's small-town Midwest," Louisa argued. "Everybody's related to everybody. Shop owners and the shoppers both. Probably had three cousins out there picking pumpkins for Tom yesterday."

"So why do you think it's so odd for Jesse to

All Roads

run into members of our family?" Betsy challenged.

"What's this guy after? Haven't you asked your-self that yet?"

"Perhaps," Betsy said, "the young man is after nothing but a little bit of kindness."

Louisa trembled. Being alone in her fear was maybe the worst part of the whole thing.

Again, she called The General into the house for the night. No way would she ever entertain another camp-out with Jesse.

This time, though, instead of sleeping in his own bed, The General would sleep next to her, where she could keep better watch on him. The General crawled into her bed, and she tucked him under her blanket before drifting off with her arm draped over his shoulder.

But when she rolled over in the earliest, haziest hours of the morning, right at the point the sun was making its first appearance, he was gone.

"Gen?" she croaked, throwing the blanket to the floor. She stomped down the stairs, calling him, finding him missing from all his usual spots—he wasn't curled up at the foot of Betsy's bed or stretched out on the rug at the base of the stairs or even sitting at the

82

back door, patiently waiting for someone to let him out.

In fact, the back door was actually cracked open.

Louisa gasped. "General!" she cried, lunging outside, the cold autumn grass stinging the soles of her bare feet.

There he was, galloping toward the creek behind the house.

Jesse waved from the side of the Winnebago, a cup of coffee in his hand.

Louisa glanced over her shoulder. Through the back screen, she could see Betsy puttering about the kitchen.

Why wasn't Betsy paying more attention to him? Letting The General sniff and roll through the grass while they picnicked within earshot was one thing. Cooking and letting him run completely free when he'd so recently been lost seemed unlike her.

Cautiously, Louisa began to move toward Jesse. She stopped abruptly when one of her bare feet landed in a soft, muddy track. That track was fresh.

Her eyes went right back to Jesse, leaning against his RV now as he watched The General race

All Roads

across the field.

When he realized she was still staring at him, he offered, "Morning" in a voice that rang overly-friendly in her ears, like an attempt to conceal whatever shenanigans he'd been up to.

Had Jesse waited for the lights to go out to coax The General downstairs? Had Jesse used the back door trick Betsy'd shown him, climbed to the second story, and hovered over Louisa while she'd slept? Then what? Had Jesse driven The General somewhere overnight? Was it the same place he'd taken The General the previous two nights? Why? What was he doing to her dog?

She needed to see The General for herself. Close up. Make sure he was okay. "General?" she called. "General! Come! Come on, boy!" She whistled.

She sighed with relief when he came galloping straight for her, tongue rippling, that excited-to-see-you grin on his face.

Louisa squatted to welcome him into her arms. His joy made her laugh—but then again, he always made her laugh, that General of hers. He was fine, obviously. Everything was fine.

He broke free from her again, off to chase after

some creature who had made the nearby brush rustle.

She would enjoy watching him play awhile. Her own coffee could wait a few more minutes.

Without thinking, she placed her hand on the nearby hood of the RV.

Her smile faded; all the horrible possibilities flooded back.

The hood was still warm.

"**H**e should stay for Thanksgiving."

Louisa gasped, dropping the strands of the braid she was still in the midst of finishing. "What are you talking about?" she asked Betsy.

The General nudged his breakfast bowl closer to the stove. In the distance, Louisa could hear water running.

"Is he taking a shower in here?" she asked.

"Doesn't seem right to send him away," Betsy insisted as the bacon snapped in her cast-iron skillet. "Thanksgiving's tomorrow. Besides, when've we ever

All Roads

had a Thanksgiving that was *just* about family? Your mom's bound to bring at least one friend—and that friend'll probably bring either a date or her kids, and you'll have Sean here this year. Tom's coming, too, and he'll surely wind up bringing his wife, a hired hand or two, and the guy who fixes his tractor."

"Jesse's not who you believe he is."

"So you're the authority on visitors now, are you?"

"He left last night. Did you know that? He's doing it every night. Where's he going? Why's he taking The General?"

"You saw The General get on the RV? You saw them leave together?" Betsy asked as she transferred her bacon strips to a plate on her warming tray.

"Did you let The General out this morning?" Louisa countered.

"You don't think Jesse could have heard The General whining to be let out? You don't think he could have opened that back door like I showed him? You don't think it's possible he's still helping you take care of that dog?"

"I'm telling you—"

"He got us those ingredients for the pie," Betsy

interrupted. "Can you honestly say it's the right thing to do to accept those ingredients and then not let him eat the pie when it's done?"

"It was just a pumpkin and some cloves," Louisa muttered.

Betsy shot her another look of disapproval as footsteps grew closer to the kitchen.

"Just the man I wanted to see," Betsy announced as Jesse emerged in clean clothes and still-soaked hair. Louisa wondered if Betsy was also doing the man's laundry.

Over Louisa's hisses of "But, but, wait," Betsy called, "You'll be here for the big feast tomorrow, right?"

"Oh," Jesse said, the invitation lighting his face. "Only if you let me bring you one more ingredient for the pie."

"Fine, fine," Betsy said, cracking an egg into her still-hot skillet of bacon grease. "Got some online sales that need to be dropped off at the post office. You can handle that, right?"

"Sure," Jesse said through an almost childlike grin.

Louisa felt like screaming—and knew, at the

87

All Roads

same time, that screaming would be useless. Was Betsy really so desperate to fill the seat at the table that had been empty for the past twenty years that she would let anyone, even a man clearly out to deceive them all, try to take it up?

Louisa'd never felt so much at odds with the entire world before.

Her wrist had also never burned so viciously before.

And she knew it was going to be up to her to get rid of this awful Jesse person. Kick him out, shoo him away, make sure that he would never dare come back again.

Katy

*H*er heart stopped when Jesse stepped from the RV. And she wasn't sure, in that moment, if she would ever get it to start again.

Betsy had called to warn her Jesse was coming to the square. Called her so that she could keep an eye out for him. Watching him more carefully now as he removed an armload of shipping boxes from his Winnebago, Katy could understand why her mother had wanted to involve the P.I. His hair was so close in color to Louisa's. Same general build, too, maybe an inch taller. But really, it was the nose, she decided. That large,

89

crooked nose could have been Photoshopped off an old picture of her father and pasted onto that young man's face.

It was hope, too, she knew. Even now. Hope could change the way the entire world looked.

She walked to the front window, watching him until he was swallowed by a door branded "USPS." Should she pretend she needed to go to the post office, too? So she could get an even better look? The Winnebago was parked so close to the front walk of her diner. Could she simply bring out a broom, sweep the front step? Use it as an excuse to say hello?

What was she going to do?

"Katy?" one of the prep cooks called out. "You okay?"

Katy reached behind her, waving her hand slightly.

Jesse stepped out of the post office, hurried across the square. He was coming back this way. She had to figure this out fast.

Only, he wasn't reaching for the driver-side door of his RV. He was passing it by. Making a beeline for her entrance.

Trembling, she hurried toward the front counter. She grabbed a mostly-empty coffee pot, and nervously busied herself with tossing the wet grounds into the trash.

Jesse slipped onto a stool at the counter. Katy placed a water glass in front of him before another waitress could claim him as her customer.

She stared at the glass for an unusually long time, afraid to raise her eyes. If she were to look at him now, this close, would she still think his hair was the same shade of blond as Louisa's? Would she still see her dad's nose? Or would she see something entirely different?

The tall drinking glass brought to mind the drive she'd taken with Mayfield the day before, out to A Stitch in Time to pick up those two orange juice glasses left over from breakfast. Louisa was gone, but who knew for how long, maybe just a few minutes, and Katy'd wanted to get out of there before she returned. She didn't want Louisa to see Mayfield. She'd remember him. That tattoo of his was hard to forget. She would wonder what was up. And Katy still felt like it was her job to shield Louisa as best she could.

"I'll put a rush on it," Mayfield had promised when Betsy'd brought out the glasses, carefully pre-

All Roads

served in Ziploc freezer bags, a name handwritten on each one: "Louisa" and "Jesse."

DNA would provide a definitive answer. But instead of offering her relief, the idea had made Katy feel sick to her stomach, and she felt every bit as sick now.

The diner water glass blurred beneath her stare as she drifted off into her favorite daydreams of the life she might have lived with James. She liked the imperfect fantasies the best, the ones involving playground bullies and curfews, as he grew, that he only ever honored by the skin of his teeth. Having to drive him to some sort of sports practice several mornings a week (there'd be awful, nasty duffel bags associated with this, and a jersey she could never seem to remember to wash). High school girlfriends she never fully approved of, and catching him smoking on the back step.

She had traveled the years in a similar fashion with Louisa, navigating the messy, smelly, loud dramas, relishing the moments of triumph and joy. But they had once been a threesome, and James's absence was still an injury, one that she had long ago learned to live with while accepting it would never quit hurting—

like learning to walk on a leg that had broken and not healed properly.

"Ma'am?"

That did it. Her head instantly bobbed up at the sound of his voice.

"I was wondering if you sold pie crust."

Katy snorted a surprised laugh. "Just the crust? No filling?"

He shrugged, his face flaming.

Katy fought the urge to touch her chest when she saw it: An eye twitch. A tic. Just like her mom had described, and just like her little boy'd exhibited every time he got upset. She remembered him rubbing his fluttering eyes with his fists while he sat on his pediatrician's examination table, his arm being swabbed in preparation for the dreaded booster shots.

"I know a lady," he said, placing his fingertips on his eyelids in an attempt to calm them down. "She's making a pie for Thanksgiving tomorrow. But I thought—if she had the dough part, at least that much wouldn't have to be messed with. It might make it easier on her." He lifted his fingers, looking straight at her to add, "And I know she eats here. Isn't she part of your family? Betsy. Remember, I met her and Louisa on your sidewalk out there? And she pointed you out, too. So. Anyway. I thought she'd like that."

Katy felt herself getting choked up. "That's nice of you."

"Oh," he said, straightening up as if a thought had suddenly come to him. "Are you already bringing the dough? I mean, it's your family. You probably are, aren't you?"

She grinned. "No, Mom—Betsy—always made the pie. It should have occurred to me to help her out like that long before now. I'm glad you thought of it. You'll be there, too, won't you?"

She held her breath as she waited for his answer.

He shrugged, his body disappearing inside his overly large hooded sweatshirt. "She invited me. She was just being nice."

Katy wanted to scoop him up into her arms. A stray. *Foster kid.* Mayfield had learned that much already by running the license plate. A lifetime in the system. Why had no one ever adopted him? Katy felt a surge of protective love for the young man; it didn't even matter to her right then if he had been hers at the beginning.

94

And really, she knew that it was more than likely that he hadn't. If Katy had learned anything over the past several years, it was that wishes didn't go around coming true all on their own, just because. Especially for her.

And yet…

There was something about him. Wasn't there? Could she put her weight on this new possibility? Or would her already broken heart and soul shatter completely under the pressure of it all?

"Wait a sec," she said, and headed into the kitchen.

She stood in front of the giant refrigerator for a while, her hand on the stainless steel handle.

Did she have the strength to do what she had the heart-thumping urge to do? Or should she grab one of the chilled balls of dough they always had on hand, put it in a container, and send this man on his way?

Lots of people had eye tics. That in itself didn't mean anything.

And yet, and yet, and yet…

Katy turned away from the fridge, stomping out through the back door. She paced, the soles of her

95

shoes scraping the cracked and buckled parking lot. Weeds poked through the gaps in the concrete.

She shook as she pulled her phone from her pocket. She felt the same way she had twenty years ago, calling her mother, calling her husband's best friend, trying to find her son.

Was that what she was doing now? Looking for her son? Or simply eliminating the possibility that this stranger could be her son? Was there a difference?

It's Thanksgiving, Katy thought as the phone on the other end rang. As though somehow, Thanksgiving was indeed a magical day. A day when dreams came true, wishes were granted. By whom, though? The president pardoned the White House turkey, but who would pardon her from what was turning out to be a lifelong sentence?

She sat down on the back step, wiping her sweaty forehead with her apron.

"Katy," Mayfield answered. "Sorry, no results yet on the DNA sample. I'll have them tonight."

Katy ended the call and fought to catch her breath, pawing the tears off her cheeks. Should she go back and talk to the young man? Convince him that everyone really did want him at Thanksgiving? Try to

96

find out some information on her own in case he didn't show? Ask him how he happened to end up in this neck of the woods, where he was headed?

This was stupid. There was no way that person in her diner could be her son. The DNA results would prove that. No question she could ask, no information she could gather, would change that. It was time to get back to putting one badly-healed broken leg in front of the other. *Just keep moving, Katy, just keep moving.*

She stood, swooning a bit against the unnatural fall heat and an unexpected dizzy feeling. And then she tugged the back door open and walked into the kitchen, straight to the fridge. She freed a ball of dough, put it in a takeout container, and hurried back into the dining area.

"Sorry about your wait," she said, her voice still thick with emotion. "For your pie," she added, handing him the container. And because she knew it was actually for her own pie, the one she would be eating tomorrow, she found herself biting her bottom lip, fighting her tears.

"How much?" he asked.

"No charge," she insisted, unable to look at him. "Happy—happy Thanksgiving. Hope to see you tomorrow."

"Thanks," he said, his tone now honestly surprised. The bell on the door rang, announcing his departure.

Katy watched through the plate glass widow beneath the "Katy's Kitchen" letters as Jesse climbed back into his RV.

She glanced down at her phone. She thought of Mayfield, of the drive they'd taken to her mother's place, of the results still pending. Yesterday, it had struck her that the only thing that seemed to have aged at all on Mayfield's muscular frame in the four years since she'd seen him last was his tattoo.

The faded but still perfectly legible ink began to hover in her mind's eye:

"Destiny."

Jesse

This was it. Jesse knew that, even as he sat behind the steering wheel of the Winnebago, covered in sweat and grimacing against his racing pulse. The end of his time with Betsy.

Night had fallen hours ago. If he didn't get a move on now, it would soon be sunrise on Thanksgiving Day.

Actually, it had seemed to him that Thanksgiving had already kicked into gear the afternoon before, when he'd returned from his trip to the square. Betsy had hung a "Closed for the Holiday" sign in

All Roads

the door, and she wasn't the only one. Nearby shops were all adorned with similar notices. Out-of-state cars were lining up, parking outside each of the houses-slash-businesses down the street.

Betsy had cheered (and *hugged* him) when he'd offered her the dough. When it had been revealed that he'd gotten it at Katy's Kitchen, the questions started in: What did he and Katy talk about? How did Katy seem?

"Seem?" he'd repeated, as Betsy had brought some spice cake into the living room to enjoy with glasses of sweet orange tea.

It was an odd question. Wasn't Katy her daughter? Why would she ask him? Couldn't she ask Katy herself tomorrow?

There it was again, that embarrassed, heavy feeling, that shameful feeling, that feeling that he was being a party crasher. An eavesdropper. And—worst of all—tolerated rather than truly accepted. He had felt the same way at the diner, talking to Katy about *her* Thanksgiving with *her* family. He couldn't do this. It was wrong. These people didn't belong to him.

"I really do appreciate the offer," he started. "But honestly, I can be on my way early in the morning, clear out before your guests—"

"*You're* my special guest," Betsy corrected. "Something called you to our town, and something keeps calling you to our family. Seems I'd be ignoring a signal from the universe if I didn't have you at my table."

He'd felt a surge of happiness. Her words wrapped themselves around his shoulders and held him close. His heart went out to Betsy, attaching itself to her like one of those silly suction cup wall-walking toys he'd once been given to play with in one temporary house or another.

She trusted him. She had from the very beginning, inviting him over and showing him how to work their back door. She'd been like The General that way.

He waited for Louisa to argue. But on the other side of the room, she simply sipped her tea, eyeing The General who snored on the couch at Jesse's side.

She was relenting. Wasn't she?

She seemed more peaceful, anyway. Somehow less likely to explode in a pure, fiery rage.

Maybe, he mused, sometime tomorrow, she might even say something to him and her words would be warm, like a pair of new gloves at the beginning of

101

the coldest season of the year.

And so he'd simply nodded an agreement. He would be there. Of course he would. They would all have Thanksgiving together.

That evening, they'd cooked a simple meal, hamburgers and fries, and Jesse admitted to himself that in the space of a few days, he had grown to love the place. Not just like. Not just appreciate. A full-blown flower of pure, undeniable affection had bloomed in his heart. He loved the pleasant feel of the sunshine in Betsy's kitchen and the wide-openness of the space behind her house, but he also loved the easy, meandering dirt path that had led to Tom's farm and the crooked smile on Katy's face as she'd handed him the dough. There was something comfortable about it all. So comfortable, in fact, that it actually almost felt, well...it felt familiar. As though part of him had always been here. Some spiritual part of him. And finally, his body had caught up. Here he was, whole.

They'd all retired early to get a bit of extra rest before the big day, the girls to their rooms, The General to Louisa's side, and Jesse to his Winnebago.

The moment he'd sat down, though, his hand had fallen to the front pocket of his jeans, where he

102

could feel the dog whistle. And a new what-if found him, too quickly to defend himself against it. One that had Betsy smiling at him after Thanksgiving dinner, saying something like, *Nice to have had you for this extended visit*, which would ring in his head like the last foster father's *'attaboy*. And the thing about Thanksgiving meals, they were always served early in the day, the afternoon rather than the evening. Which meant there would be plenty of time left after the last bite of pumpkin pie for him to get a move on. Why, he could make some real headway before nightfall! The entire family would wave him goodbye, no need for him to stick around yet another night. The back door would be locked. The General would be lost to him for good.

The scenario offered a cold reality check for sure.

Comfortable. Familiar. They seemed such empty words now. Or, more accurately, like lies he'd told himself, some way—yet again—to make it seem reasonable for him to stay.

But *stay*, as always, was temporary.

That was the way you always put it to a dog, didn't you? "Stay, stay," meaning, *Sit here a minute*.

He felt the old barriers again. The distinct line

103

All Roads

between *you* and *us*.

And he'd stepped from the RV with the dog whistle pressed to his lips.

oster kids had to take whatever came their way. But Jesse was a grown-up now, on his own, able to avoid being shoved around anymore.

That was what he'd been telling himself ever since The General had come downstairs, summoned by the whistle. He'd put The General in the passenger seat and had slipped behind the wheel, intending to do it, finally. Just pull away for good.

Only, it hadn't been as easy as that. Instead, he'd sat for almost an hour, staring at the stars sparkling on the opposite side of the windshield. He needed to quit dragging his feet like this. Any minute now, Louisa could roll over, find The General missing, and come running outside.

"Play-pretend's fun, but we've got to go," he told The General, who in return offered Jesse a serious expression, one that dragged his jowls down in a way that made him seem a little heartbroken.

"I'm sure you'd like to have one more Thanksgiving here, but I promise to buy you some turkey and gravy from a deli in the very next town we come to, okay?"

The General snorted.

"I will. Honest. Real food. Heck, I'll even learn to cook for you. I'd do that for you. Okay?"

The General stared.

"I've got the entirety of this town—and about three of the neighboring towns—all mapped out in my head. I know it now like—well. I just know it. After all this driving around in the daylight. I'll be able to go straight to the highway this time. And then…"

Why was it so hard to start the engine?

All roads lead to home.

There it was again. That dumb proclamation Betsy'd made. The words kept finding him, but why? Because he ached to belong. Because he liked the notion of being drawn here, like it was his destiny. Like maybe, just maybe, there really was a place on this earth that was right for him. The kind of place he should stay, and not temporarily. A permanent place, that smelled

All Roads

not like newspapers, like that last foster home, but like giant towering trees that had spent decade after decade growing in the same spot of earth. Trees that still had thick, viable roots. The kind of roots that would feed them through several more decades.

He liked the idea of some force in the world making every road he took swirl right back to Betsy.

He also liked the idea because it made it easier if he didn't have a choice in the matter. Almost like he was a child or a dog. All he could do was obey, follow the road that kept leading him back to where he'd started.

But the world wasn't demanding anything.

And Jesse wasn't a child.

Jesse had to make a choice.

He put his hand on the key. But the twist of an invisible knife pierced him under his ribs. The same stabbing pain he'd felt watching The General run away.

He growled and beat the wheel. Why couldn't he just *go?*

He wanted to stay. He couldn't stay. He wanted The General. And he would always feel guilty for taking him from Louisa. That guilt would never really go away, not after he'd been shown so many kindnesses.

The guilt would no doubt taint their being together. It would remain a sore spot deep inside. And maybe, sometimes, thick gnarly scar tissue could make a person feel tough—like they'd gone through something awful and lived to tell about it. But taking The General would never make Jesse feel tough. It would make him feel mean. Hateful. Even regretful.

He had never once thought of himself in those terms. Expendable, at times. Lonesome always as he'd bounced from family to family, tumbling down the street like a discarded candy wrapper being tossed about by the wind. But he'd never been ashamed of who he was.

And yet...

Quit this, Jesse. Quit thinking in circles. Quit driving in circles. You've got to get on with your life. You know you've got to leave. It's leave or lose The General forever.

All Roads

Katy

The phone rang after midnight. Katy gasped and grabbed the phone off the pillow beside her. The same cell phone she'd been staring at for the past hour rather than sleeping.

By the time she pressed it to her face, she was already crying. Terrified.

Only one person could possibly be calling her at this hour. And yet, the sound of Mayfield's voice hit her like a magnitude-8 earthquake. It peeled back twenty years. It peeled back scabs. It rebroke the broken leg she'd been hobbling around on all these years.

She was hurt and she was bleeding, and all the horrible words she didn't get to say out loud to her husband were floating back up, scraping against every last one of her raw emotions:

Why did you do it? To hurt me. Okay. But didn't you care about your own son? Did you really give him away? How could you? What kind of person does that? Did you forget your daughter existed? Did you hate me that much? Where is our son now? Where is he?

Mayfield kept talking, but she couldn't process it all. Aftershocks were still making the ground beneath her unsteady.

The DNA results were back. They had to be. But now his words were coming at her, flying so fast—zipping like bottle rockets, flying off before she could grasp them. And they were dangerous, anyway, those words. Certain to burn holes straight through her if she tried to catch them.

And all around her, the world kept on shaking...

She squeezed her eyes shut. Was Jesse another scam artist? Or did his eye tic really mean something? Did he really look like her daughter, or was that her imagination?

Worse yet: Why didn't she already know who

109

All Roads

Jesse was? Why didn't she have some sort of radar or instinct or motherly *anything* that could have convinced her, when he came to her diner and sat mere inches away, whether or not he was her own son?

Mayfield's voice grew louder as he repeated the same phrase over and over.

"Wait," she begged. "Slow down. What are you saying?"

He started over, but she couldn't have heard him right. In her mind, the real world was all mixed up with the dream world, the one in which her son came home.

He knew who Jesse was. That much got through to her, made sense to her.

"Tell me that again," she begged. "Start from the beginning."

Louisa

She had been pacing the front porch for an hour. Waiting for Jesse to pull away, take off, embark on whatever he was doing every single night. She was going to catch him in the act.

At least, that had been the plan.

Now, though, she was beginning to wonder what, exactly, was taking him so long to get started.

She'd already been awake—arms folded behind her head as she waited for the squeak of the kitchen door or the shuffle of feet on the stairs—when The General had jumped out of bed. Instead of calling him

111

All Roads

back, Louisa had gone to her bedroom window and watched through a gap in the sheer, filmy curtains as Jesse'd walked closer to their house, moonlight shining on a metal object he was holding to his mouth. A dog whistle, surely. It had to be, judging by the way The General kept following along after Jesse once he'd freed him from the back door, almost like he was the Pied Piper.

Louisa'd exploded with fury as Jesse put The General in his RV. But only for a moment. In its place, the calm assurance she'd been carrying ever since she'd made her decision earlier that afternoon took over. She was going to tackle this thing head-on. She'd known that much even as she'd sipped Betsy's orange tea.

She'd grabbed her phone, raced down the stairs and through the front door, taking care not to wake Betsy along the way.

She wanted to do this herself. And she didn't want Betsy turning it all around, scolding Louisa and convincing Jesse not to go.

No, Louisa would confront Jesse, force him to return her dog and make it clear that if she ever saw him in town again, she would go to the police. *Theft, fraud*—and any other charge she could possibly

112

think of. In a smaller town, charges often held as much weight as actual convictions.

Adrenaline overtook any last-minute fear as she geared up for the fight of her life.

She paced the boards between the door and the front step, angrily turning the phone over and over in her hand, waiting for the RV to putter around the side of the house.

The longer she stood, the colder Louisa felt. She wished she'd grabbed her robe or at least Betsy's jacket, the one she always left on the hook beside the door.

What was going on in that RV? Why had she let The General go? What if Jesse was truly rotten— and had never cared for the dog at all? What if he hurt him now? What was wrong with her? Was she so anxious to prove herself right about Jesse that she put The General in harm's way?

She had to do something. Quickly.

She'd just started to step off the porch when the sound of an engine cranking to life scratched against the night air.

Finally. It was happening. Jesse was making a run for it—with her dog.

All Roads

She raced across the front yard, the cold dew drops stinging the soles of her feet. Shoes—she'd also forgotten her shoes. How could she have been so stupid?

She had no time now to grab them. But it was no matter. She'd gladly endure a few cuts and scrapes for The General.

She sprinted across the lawn, ready to stand her ground in the driveway. When Jesse circled around the house, he would surely use the driveway to coast into the street.

The RV slowly lumbered into view, headlights still off. Closer and closer. What was he doing? Why wasn't he slowing down? Why was he driving right for her?

Jesse couldn't see her. Not with the headlights black. He didn't know she was there.

"Hey!" she tried. But the RV kept rolling forward; her choice was either to move or be squashed.

"Hey, you!" she shouted, louder this time, as she darted aside just enough to avoid being hit squarely by the ungainly Winnebago.

She couldn't be sure, but it seemed her voice may have tugged his foot from the gas pedal for a moment. The RV lurched again, as though Jesse had decided to ignore her and speed away.

"Wait! No, no, no! Please stop!" Louisa screamed. At that moment, about to lose The General for good, she found herself chin-deep in the quicksand of remorse that had been threatening to suffocate her for decades. Why had she pouted and cried the night her dad had shown up, announcing he wanted to take James for a ride? Only James, not her? How could she have glared at her twin because their dad was sitting on the edge of his bed, telling him to hurry up so they could go on some grand journey beneath the stars? Why had she been so stupidly jealous that her dad had meant only to wake her brother, and there she was, obviously awakened by accident?

"Go back to sleep, sweetie," her dad had hissed through the moonlit bedroom.

Filled with anger and hurt feelings, she'd stuck out her tongue and pulled the covers over her eyes to tell them, *Go. Who needs either of you, anyway?*

It didn't matter that she was only four. She still remembered the night clearly. She still hated herself for not stopping it. It would have been so easy. In her anger at not being chosen, she could have thrown a

All Roads

regular four-year-old's tantrum, making far more noise than her dad had counted on. She could have called out, "Mo—oom!" in that way little kids did, that tattling singsong: *I'm telling on you!*

Instead, as it was, she simply went back to sleep. When she'd gone down to breakfast, her mother had asked, "Where's your brother?" and Louisa had shrugged in a *Who cares? He's a big meanie* kind of way. When her mother's eyes got wide and she started making phone calls, Louisa'd known something was really wrong.

But in all honesty, hadn't she known before that? The very fact that her father had shown up in the middle of the night—dressed—and wanting to go for a ride with James was just plain weird. Even at four, she'd sensed that, hadn't she? She could have saved her brother.

But she hadn't. She'd let him go.

Now, here she was again, in the midst of a situation she knew was wrong, about to let some stranger drive away with The General? Had she learned nothing? At that moment, it felt to Louisa that she was repeating the same mistake, reliving the same scene all over again.

116

Louisa squeezed her eyes shut and clamped her hands into fists at her sides. She opened her mouth and out it poured, finally: the scream that had been festering inside of her for the past twenty years. A scream of fear and pain and regret. A scream of wondering what kind of person she really was, deep inside, because she was finally admitting to herself that she'd let it happen all those years ago. A scream that confessed she could have changed things. A scream exploding with guilt. A scream that said if she had put up a fight and demanded to go with them, at least James wouldn't have been alone. And she wouldn't have had to replay daily the events of that night so long ago. The little girl still buried inside her was screaming, too, begging to know why her father had taken him, not her. Did he think it would be a greater punishment for her mother? Did he think James would be missed more? Was he her mother's favorite?

Why, why, why, why?

The brake lights glowed solidly against the night.

Louisa grew quiet, finally, her cry still echoing faintly.

Before the RV could get going again, she raced

117

toward the front of it, aiming her phone at the windshield. She called out, her voice hoarse and injured, "I've got you. *Thief!*"

She was so scared. And so desperate. And so furious.

"You're stealing The General! I'm recording it! I have pictures of your license plate. Give me my dog, and you get out of here and never come back. Never! You do that, and I won't—press—charges. Just. Give me back my dog. Okay?"

Spit was flying as she spoke, and she was shaking so hard, she could barely keep her phone at eye level. In her heart, she wasn't just stopping Jesse or rescuing The General. In her heart, she was also saving James. She was wrenching him away from their father—like she should have done all those years ago. She was changing everything. Putting it all back to the way it should have been.

The RV door opened. Jesse stepped outside. "Louisa," he said, in a tone that indicated he knew he was cornered. "I'm sorry. So sorry."

"Sorry?" she croaked. "Easy to say when you've been caught."

Her eyes roved toward the house; lights shone

118

in windows on the first and second stories. Betsy was up.

"Please," Jesse begged. "Don't tell Betsy. Okay? Please?"

"You've got to be kidding!" Louisa barked as the front door flapped open. Betsy called out to them, waving her arms. She wasn't just shouting their names, though. She was rattling on, talking in wild sentences—trying to tell them something. But what?

"Please," Jesse said again. "The General's yours. I only—I loved him so much, I couldn't…"

Jesse took a giant step backward, his hand reaching out for the open RV door.

The world around them intensified: An engine grew louder as it approached. Headlights brightened. From the front yard, Betsy's voice turned higher pitched.

Jesse took another backward step.

"You need to get out of here," Louisa growled. "*Without* my dog."

When the pain hit, Louisa's fingers opened. She yelped as her phone slipped from her fingers and shattered against the driveway.

Of all the times for her birthmark to start hurt-

119

ing. It burned with an intensity that bent her at the waist, buckled her knee.

"Are you okay?" Jesse asked, reaching for her.

Louisa gasped. In the wash of headlights, with Jesse's hand on hers and his sweatshirt sleeve pulled back slightly, she saw it clearly.

Jesse had a birthmark. On his wrist. Exactly like her own.

"I know," Betsy said, panting now beside them. "I saw it, too. Even that first day, it seemed like proof."

In her shock, Louisa let out a quick, surprised laugh. It was the only sound she knew how to make at that moment. This couldn't be happening. Maybe she was in the midst of some vivid dream; maybe she was still in bed, The General snoring beside her.

No—this was real. The crisp air around her and the rough driveway under her bare feet and the harsh glare of the headlights were anything but imagined.

And there they were, before her eyes, side by side: two matching birthmarks.

Jesse cocked his head, looking at Louisa in a startled way.

"Her laugh sounds familiar to you, doesn't it?" Betsy asked. "Oh, how the two of you used to chase each other, behind my house, through Tom's garden rows, just laughing all the way."

"Not me," Jesse said, shaking his head, obviously confused and shaken.

Betsy was crying at this point. "Yes," she said. "Louisa and—"

But Louisa interrupted, wanting to be the first person to say his name out loud.

"James," she whispered. "It's you."

All Roads

The General

Even then, when The General was still sitting in the RV, he knew that everyone involved would wind up telling this story in a way that made it seem some magical force had been instrumental in bringing them all together. They would maybe even throw in a few of their big fancy human words like "providential" or "fate." Betsy would be a little more folksy about it. She'd haul out the same phrases she'd been using lately. That stuff about the heart leading a person or the right roads calling. James—or Jesse, maybe he would still hang on to the name he'd grown the most used to—would talk about feeling drawn here.

None of them would ever recognize who had really orchestrated the whole thing.

But that was pretty much life when you were a dog. Humans called your name and expected you to come. They said they "rescued" you. They considered you their companion, maybe. Their workmate. But never, not once in The General's life, had anyone ever stopped to realize that he'd had an impact on the turn of events that played out in front of them.

So it would really be no surprise when they failed to recognize his hard work here.

In truth, his work had started in earnest nearly three weeks ago. He'd ridden along with Louisa to a neighboring town. A delivery trip, where she would drop off yarn to sell at a local craft shop. He didn't mind visiting the store. As always, it was good to get the wind in his face as they sped down the highway, and besides, the owner kept bones behind the counter. The good ones made out of sweet potatoes.

He had crunched away at his usual treat and barked at the door. Louisa liked to shoot the leisurely breeze with the owner of this particular shop, and he wasn't in the mood to hang around inside too long.

All Roads

The carpet in the store was a strange texture, and it made his belly itch.

Besides, there was a patch of grass in front of the resale shop across the street just begging to be dug up. He couldn't wait to get his toenails into the earth beneath the late-blooming fall strawflowers.

He had really started to get into it, tossing loose dirt all over the place—including himself—when the smell floated into his nose. It made him stop everything and walk into the street, stick his snout in the air as he tried to figure out which direction it was coming from.

Usually, The General couldn't put a single toe in the street without somebody hollering at him to get back. Like he needed humans to remind him the street was dangerous. He knew it was dangerous. Danger had its own unique scent.

Actually, everything in the world had a scent. Oh, sure, places like parks and street corners and the insides of buildings did. That was a given. Katy's diner smelled like hunger and the elementary school smelled like rules and the post office smelled like surprises.

But people had their own smells, too.

He had never been sure how humans could

124

stand to go through life missing out on so many tantalizing aromas. They recognized only the heavy-handed scents: onions and roses and soap and pie in the oven. If their noses were worth anything, they would never have to go around spritzing themselves with so much stinky aftershave and perfume in order to give themselves something new to sniff.

As a pup, The General had learned to recognize people based on their smell. To be sure, humans often smelled like what they spent the most time doing: Katy smelled of pot roast and the handmade sausages she liked to fill his belly with. Louisa sometimes smelled like the sheep she'd just helped shear...but humans also smelled of emotions.

Dogs can smell fear on a person, that was a saying The General had often heard. Didn't anyone ever stop to think that dogs could also smell their sadness or regret or ambition? Happiness or excitement or disappointment? Didn't any of them ever wonder how it was that their own dog happened to sense when they needed someone to curl up with on the couch after that particularly brutal breakup or being fired?

Still. The smell coming to him that day. It was Louisa's.

All Roads

Only, she was inside the craft store, blabbering away. He could see her through the plate glass. And this smell was wafting from the opposite direction.

"Hey!" a voice called out. The General turned; the owner of the resale shop, a middle-aged woman with a pointy face and her hands on her hips, stood right beside The General's brand-new hole. "Hey, you! You dig up my flowers?"

The General knew he couldn't exactly deny it. After all, he was covered in the evidence: gritty dirt clung to his neck, falling under the collar Louisa had stitched for him herself. It was in his ears and around his mouth.

"C'mere, you no-good mutt!" the owner shouted. Then, when it looked like The General wasn't going to hop right to it, she glanced in the direction of the craft store, cupped her mouth with her hand, and shouted, "Louisa!"

The General took off, as was his habit when he knew he was in trouble. Better to let a human get a little worried about you, cool down, *then* come when you were called. By that point, the vase you'd knocked over or the mud you'd gotten on the kitchen floor was all cleaned up, and the humans were ready to turn the

126

page.

But as he'd raced around the corner, the smell got stronger.

He swore it smelled exactly like Louisa, minus the smell of the sheep. Her own identical potpourri of sadness and fear and the slight lingering twinge of hope. It smelled like her own beginning, her history, her mystery.

And it was coming from a strange man carrying a plastic shopping bag and unlocking the door of an RV. The General trotted right up to that stranger, because he already knew he wasn't really a stranger at all.

He lifted a paw in greeting. And the man grinned in that funny way humans did. Their expressions were always so over-the-top. You didn't see dogs going around stretching their faces willy-nilly—mad, sad, happy.

That smell, though...

The General cocked his head to the side and gave Jesse a look that he intended to say, "Huh. So *that's* who you are. I've heard plenty about you." Mostly, he'd listened to the story during the times he and Louisa had house-sat for Katy. Louisa had hauled out

All Roads

her mother's scrapbooks and curled up with him on Katy's bed. Pointed to pictures from newspapers and told him, "That's my brother."

Jesse completely misinterpreted his greeting, though. Par for the course for a human.

But he did invite The General into his RV. And, to be totally upfront, Jesse also smelled like safety. Honesty. Which was why The General climbed aboard. Together, they'd sped away.

The unloading of secrets happened pretty quickly after that. Even faster than it had started with Louisa, who had come for him when he was still a pup. Back then, she had been more concerned with The General's well-being: getting him fed properly, finding a bed he liked, getting him used to a leash—and then getting him trained so that she wouldn't constantly have to rely on a leash, so she could trust him to run through the fields behind her house and then return when his name went floating through the air.

Yes, people always liked to unload their confessions onto dogs. Kids and grown-ups alike were all-too-willing to reveal their deepest, darkest secrets. The General, at this point, already knew all of Betsy's and Katy's and Louisa's—and Sean's and half of Betsy's regular customers'. Even Pete the walking mailman liked to sit on the curb, scratch The General's back, and tell him about the latest disagreement he'd had with his wife. The General knew all about Maddy, too, the eleven-year-old girl who lived next door to Betsy, who wasn't doing so well in science. Who had, quite recently, tried to goad him into eating her test paper with the giant D- on it.

Yes, dogs knew what people were up to. Because they could smell it, and because people were all the time blabbing to them.

Jesse, it seemed, hadn't had a single living creature to talk to in—maybe ever. And he had eagerly told The General everything. *Foster kid.*

The General wondered why no one had ever adopted him. He was a good guy. Heck, The General'd been adopted right off the bat by Louisa, no shelter or foster families at all. He was lucky that way. He wished Jesse had been as lucky.

They'd circled for two weeks. It had almost turned into torture. Not that he didn't like Jesse, but he was getting serious indigestion from all the cheap kibble. He wasn't used to dog food, frankly. The fake bacon treats offered a bit of a break, but even those

All Roads

things were borderline inedible. And the gas station burritos Jesse lived on himself smelled wickedly rotten. Worse than trash trucks, as far as The General was concerned. He ached to get back to Katy's sausages.

So for two long weeks, he kept steering Jesse, as dogs always steered people. Already, in the two years he'd known Louisa, he'd steered her away from one bad boyfriend, toward living full-time with her grandmother, and to and from a host of other, less important things.

For a while there, he'd halfway suspected she'd had an inkling as to what he was up to, what with naming him The General. Like she was well aware he was giving the orders, calling the shots. But, no, it had been tongue-in-cheek, a joke, this little cute puppy suddenly requiring so much care. *As demanding as a drill sergeant*, that was how she'd put it. She had no idea what he was really up to with his well-timed nuzzles or his reactions to new people on their morning walks. (He felt great pride, too, at having convinced Louisa to give Sean an honest shot.) Still, though—Louisa was smart and a bit more leery than others, and he had to make an extra effort to keep his work on the down-low.

With Jesse, he learned quickly that he needed

to be more direct. Blunt at times. When it looked like Jesse was about to steer toward a highway that would lead to a neighboring state, a well-placed bark or pawing at the door could get him immediately back on the right track. Once, at a park, he'd knocked a paper map from Jesse's hand and shredded it. He'd really torn it to pieces, acting like it was a game until Jesse'd finally laughed in the way that said he didn't mind at all that The General was being destructive when he was also being adorable. Cuteness always, in a human's world, seemed to win out over everything else.

Still. Two weeks. And he hadn't managed to get Jesse to steer his crazy RV down the street that would lead them back to A Stitch in Time. So when they pulled into the gas station and he smelled her—Louisa—her scent pouring straight from the town square, of course he'd had to jump into action and make a run for it.

He'd known, even as he was still escaping through the rolled-down RV window, that Jesse would follow.

He'd known, too, that after Jesse walked inside Louisa and Betsy's house, he wouldn't really want to leave. Why would he? This was the very family he'd

All Roads

been aching for.

Oh, sure, in the days following Jesse's arrival, The General'd had some welcome help along the way—what had drawn him to Tom's pumpkin patch? To Esther's place? Heck, what had drawn Jesse to the area so that he and The General could meet in the first place? So much of it remained a mystery. But in his experience, dogs were generally much more comfortable curling up next to mysteries than humans were. Humans had an annoying habit of having to explain everything, attaching wild stories to events they didn't completely understand. It didn't even seem to matter to them that most of their explanations were plain wrong. He guessed it was the result of being cursed with such dull senses. With the inability to adequately smell or hear or otherwise soak up the world around them, they'd all retreated into their own heads.

Regardless, The General'd had a much easier time of steering Jesse back to Betsy's place each night than he'd had trying to steer him to her house to begin with. Jesse would grow sleepy, which meant he had very little fight in him. He could no longer resist daydreaming about a real home or thinking about the tiniest green sprouts of affection he'd begun to feel for

132

the people he was trying to steal The General from.

Those were exactly the kind of green sprouts that The General did not, in any way, have any desire to dig up.

They were also the kind of green sprouts that meant Jesse was looking for any excuse to head back to Betsy's place. The General was more than happy to provide those excuses—all while navigating from the passenger seat.

Yes, the once broken-apart family had been brought together again because of a dog. Louisa and Jesse would eventually readily agree to it. They would tell such a story once the dust settled, but they would mean only that it was an ongoing disagreement over who owned The General that had made them look closely, finally realize who they all were to each other.

The General's efforts would go forever unrecognized.

And that was perfectly fine, The General

thought as he lingered in the RV, still trying to give them all a moment to work some of this out themselves.

But it was looking a little like they might need him again. It was after midnight—the time of day when humans seemed naturally frazzled—and the RV was parked at a crazy crooked angle in the middle of the driveway, and Betsy and Louisa and Jesse were all talking in that confused way, all those competing voices, each one insisting theirs was the only one everyone should listen to.

Would they ever calm back down? Were they going to need his assistance again?

The General shook his head, sending his long ears clapping. Oh, they were making such a terrible, painful noise—all those loud, screeching voices! His head was pulsing. Yet people yelled at dogs when they barked too much.

The Winnebago's door had been left standing ajar—so The General decided to jump down the steps. A car pulled into the driveway, headlights harsh and stinging his eyes.

The car stopped abruptly; Katy's silhouette emerged and she raced forward, her own car door still

134

open, her cardigan flapping out from her sides. People had a strange way of running, too. So floppy, their arms swinging about like wings that didn't work.

"James," Louisa repeated as Katy joined them, gasping for air.

Katy let out a whimper at the sound of her son's name. "I know. His DNA matches yours," she told Louisa. "I called Mom to tell her."

Betsy smiled. "It had to be. He just had to be..."

"Wait," Jesse said, trying to pull away. "My DNA? What is this?"

The General cocked his head, watching as Louisa tugged on Jesse's hand, twisting his arm so that his birthmark was easier to see.

"How did you know my real name?" Jesse asked. "My first name, I mean. I've always gone by Jesse."

"Not always," Katy said.

"How do you know?"

The General sighed. It took people so painfully long to catch up. The General already knew that Katy was helping Jesse latch onto his vague memory of affection (*could be either a biological parent or an early foster*),

135

All Roads

and he knew by the look on Louisa's face that her wrist had stopped burning. And that Betsy was looking at Katy and trying not to grab hold of her in the tightest hug imaginable and—

"Who are you, exactly?" Jesse asked.

A tear filled the corner of Katy's eye. When she smiled, her cheeks bulged upward and the tear was pushed out. "Your mom," she whispered.

Jesse shook. "You can't. No one knows who that is. My story—files—gone."

"I know your story," Katy insisted. "The beginning of it, anyway."

When their voices started in again, all at the same time, The General offered a short insistent bark.

They all glanced down at him, chuckling. Touching his head. That did it; his bark calmed them down, ended that awful high-pitched screeching.

"Jesse, why don't you get the RV parked for the night and turn that engine off?" Betsy said. "You, too, Katy. Shut your door. Turn off the headlights. I'll make some coffee."

Jesse and Katy complied; Louisa slapped her leg to call The General close.

But he was already racing up the front walk,

136

toward the door, anxious to get them all inside.

In the kitchen, the four of them gathered around the table, happily shocked, gleefully unsure. Betsy started repeating something about "Thanks and giving," and The General knew she wasn't just trying to fill up the quiet kitchen.

He dropped down to the linoleum, ears perked. There would be stories to tell today. Lots of them. At the end of it, four disconnected threads would be joined into a single piece of fabric. And they would agree there was good reason Jesse had never been adopted: because his family was still out there waiting for him. All this time. They'd never given him up.

The General noticed they released slightly different scents than they ever had, strong enough to change the way the entire house smelled.

Oh, the house was usually a regular ever-changing kaleidoscope of scents; after all, it was attached to the shop—so many comings and goings, so many strangers traipsing through.

But this was different. The house had never smelled like this before.

The General stuck his nose in the air, not even sure what to call it at first. On the road, even smells fly-

137

ing by at forty miles an hour had been easily recognizable—dumpsters and burger joints and burning yard waste.

This, though—it was a mix of relief and anguish, of well-worn familiarity swirling with the brand-new. Almost like the smell of ancient compost mingling with freshly tilled earth.

Blended all together, though, it was particularly sniff-worthy. Maybe his favorite of all. Better than bacon frying or Louisa's hair or snow on pine trees. Yes, definitely—it was by far the best that had ever tingled inside The General's nose.

He sat, panting and staring happily at the people he had brought together. And he knew, without a doubt, what he was finally savoring at that moment, for the very first time. He knew what to call it: a word that he had heard humans use over and over, but had never quite seemed right. Not to him. Not for this house. Not until now.

It was, quite simply, the glorious, one-of-a-kind smell of home.

Also by Holly Schindler

Just in Time for the Holidays

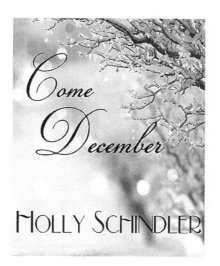

Natalie is new to town, and feels invisible and painfully alone...until a mysterious stranger in a cemetery changes everything.

Available at Amazon

Also by Holly Schindler

Just in Time for the Holidays

When a series of devastating Christmas Eve misadventures conspire against her, Mallory is forced to re-examine everything—her beliefs, her dreams, her own definition of success. What will Mallory choose? What will she discover about herself? About her destiny?

Available at Amazon

Also by Holly Schindler

Just in Time for the Holidays

New in 2017:

Welcome to Ruby's, where the Christmas spirit is alive and well.

Available at Amazon

Holly Schindler is a hybrid author of traditionally and independently published books for readers of all ages. She writes in a wide variety of genres (contemporary, romance, women's fiction, thriller, children's, YA, humor, etc.); her work has received starred reviews in Booklist and Publishers Weekly, has won silver and gold medals in ForeWord Reviews Book of the Year and the IPPY Awards, respectively, has been featured on Booklist's Best First Novels for Youth and School Library Journal's What's Hot in YA, and has been a PW Pick of the Week.

142

Find the full list of Schindler's independent and traditional releases, sign up for her newsletters, or get in touch at her author site:

HollySchindler.com

Connect online:

Twitter: @holly_schindler

Facebook: facebook.com/HollySchindlerAuthor

Made in the USA
Middletown, DE
10 December 2018